ACKNOWLEDGMENTS

Thank you to all the supporters of dreams in the world.

BOOKS BY NEVADA YORK

Caught Up

Mahogany's Revelation

DEDICATION

This book is dedicated to those who continue to be eager and vigilant for the arrival of our Lord.

CHARACTERS

Damien Andrews- EMPLOYEE PHOENIX TECHNOLOGY, EX-BOYFRIEND OF MAHOGANY FOX

Steven Eisenberg-MEMBER OF SHTIAH ROCK ASSEMBLY

Pastor Ethan- PASTOR OF CALVARY FELLOWSHIP CHURCH

Ollie Exum- SUPERVISOR OF *THE NORTH CAROLINA POST*

Nicole Hunt- PERSONAL ASSISTANT TO MICHAEL REED

David Ibraham-POPE CANDIDATE

Gabriel Kaufman- FOUNDER OF SHTIAH ROCK ASSEMBLY

Joseph Levine- CHIEF RABBINATE OF ISRAEL

Omar Miller- STAFF WRITER FOR *THE NORTH CAROLINA POST*, HUSBAND OF SHANICE MILLER

Shanice Miller-BEST FRIEND OF MAHOGANY FOX

Joshua Neuman- MEMBER OF CALVARY FELLOWSHIP CHURCH

Lieutenant David Peck- OWNER OF STONES UNCOVERED DETECTIVE AGENCY

Dawn Price-EMPLOYEE OF STONES UNCOVERED

Michael Reed-CHIEF EXECUTIVE OFFICER of PHOENIX TECHNOLOGY

Trent Royal-EX-BOYFRIEND OF DAWN PRICE

Bart Wendell-CHIEF FINANCIAL OFFICER of PHOENIX TECHNOLOGY

Roy Dean Williams- PRESIDENT OF THE UNITED STATES

"But of that day and hour no one knows, neither the angels in heaven, nor the Son, but only the Father. Take heed, watch and pray; for you do not know when the time is."

Mark 14, Verse 32-33.

"And he causes all, both small and great, rich and poor, free and slave, to receive a mark on their right hand or on their foreheads, and that no one who has the mark or the name of the beast, may buy or sell except one who has the mark or the name of the beast, or the number of his name."

Revelations 13, Verse 16-17.

Chapter One

Jake was nervous. Too much time had passed without her touch. He slowly pulled her closer to him.

"I'm sorry that I ever tried to hurt you," he whispered.

The tension between the two of them was palpable. He nibbled on the nape of her neck, sending shivers up her spine. Mahogany could feel every detail of his body against hers. Jake tugged impatiently at the buttons on her blouse.

Cradling her head between his hands, he absorbed every detail of her face and leisurely moved in on her lips. A deep moan erupted in the back of her throat from the pressure of his mouth. Jake's hand delicately caressed her skin beneath her blouse, leaving a scorching mark wherever his hand touched. Mahogany closed her eyes from the pleasure.

He rolled her over onto the bed, completely covering her body with his. He pressed his lips closer against hers, making a tight seal. When she tried to move her lips for air, Jake held her head in a firm grip. She pushed against his chest, but it garnered no reaction from him. He pinned Mahogany's arms above her head and used his body weight to crush her. Panicked, she opened her eyes to find his eyes bearing directly through her soul. Her lungs began to burn from the lack of air. The room slowly turned black. If she could only take one breath…

Mahogany awoke with a start. She quickly flicked on the lamp near her nightstand and placed her hand over her heart, the fast beating echoed throughout her bedroom. When would the nightmares stop? It had been a little over two years since the incident. A deranged person tried to murder her and it was called an "incident."

"Mama."

Lucas called Mahogany from her thoughts. She had given birth to a beautiful baby boy. Lucas Andrews. He was seven pounds, eight ounces. During her pregnancy she had gained over forty pounds and Damien was with her every step of the way—only as a friend, he wasn't ready for more. Mahogany was fine with his decision. The past they once shared was over. Once upon a time, Damien Andrews held the key to her heart. Yet, she found out the hard way that Damien was a key collector.

He cheated on her in more ways than she could count. But that was then and this is now. She needed to focus on herself and her son. Lucas had his mother's eyes and his father's long eyelashes.

Everyone mentioned how much Lucas resembled Damien, joking that Damien could not deny Lucas was his son even if he wanted to. He had everything of Damien's, right down to his dimples. They had celebrated his first birthday last week at Planet Kids. She smiled to herself remembering how Damien appeared more afraid of the kiddy spaceship ride than Lucas did. The mixture of Damien's fake screams and Lucas' giggles was an image Mahogany would never forget.

Mahogany entered Lucas' room. They painted his wall a calm blue color. She read in a magazine that the color blue helped children subconsciously relax. How much of it was true, she didn't know, but it had a positive effect on her whenever she entered his room. Plush teddy bears were in each corner of the ceiling.

"Hey, baby cakes," she whispered.

Rising, he pulled himself up and extended his arms in a plea to be removed from his crib.

"Ma," he said as she picked him up.

Mahogany returned to her bedroom and placed him on the thick comforter located on her bed. He laid back down without hesitation. Her thoughts drifted back to her nightmare. She could never stop thinking about Jake. How could one person want to take another person's life? According to Jake, the reason was simple. His mother loathed the fact that he was attracted to Mahogany—a black woman. To honor the memory of his late mother, he directed his own self-hatred towards

Mahogany. It wasn't until several months ago in her trauma group that Mahogany understood that she will truly never get an answer which satisfies her. Nor, will she blame herself for Jake's mental anguish.

Jake Reeves. The time they spent together in high school seemed like a blur and the times she did remember with Jake were less than impressionable. Mahogany remembered speaking to him from time to time, and smiling at him in the hallways. He was also a regular at her lunch table. He never rubbed her the wrong way, but things were distant between the two of them.

Until that night, she never knew why he tried to murder her. He would have succeeded if Lieutenant Peck and Dawn had not shown up in the nick of time. Jake was dead, she personally saw his bloody body. Mahogany pressed her eyes shut, letting that revelation sink in. Although time had passed, the torturous event remained fresh in her memory. The phone rang, interrupting her thoughts.

"Hello."

"Hey girl," It was her best friend Shanice. She and her husband, Omar, had reconciled. Omar had matured into the perfect doting husband. Gone were his PlayStation video playing days. He and Shanice were both trying to keep their marriage together. It was a daily challenge but they were determined to hold on to what they had.

"Don't tell me," sighed Mahogany. "You won't be able to visit the church. This will make it the second time Joshua has invited us and you've cancelled both times."

"I'm sorry," groaned Shanice. "But Omar is tripping saying how he needs to go out and I don't have a sitter for Chloe."

Mahogany didn't have the foggiest idea what Shanice's problem was, but this was the second time that she cancelled plans they made.

"Shanice, c'mon, we've been planning this for weeks." "I promise," declared Shanice. "I'll make it up to you."

"Can't you let Dawn watch Chloe? She'll be baby-sitting Lucas. Just bring her over and we can still go."

"No, no. I'm not trying to rock the boat, Mahogany. I'll get up with you later, okay. Don't be upset with me."

"I won't."

"Thanks for understanding. It will be my treat next week," finished

Shanice.

Mahogany heard a resounding click in her ear before the doorbell rang. There was something Shanice wasn't telling her. She saw Dawn's image through the window. After opening the door, she whispered to Dawn that Lucas was still asleep.

Dawn Price still looked the same, but the shooting caused a lot to change on the inside. She viewed the world differently. No longer did she give people the benefit of the doubt. From experience, she learned to take what people said with a grain of salt. Gone were the days when honesty was considered a fine attribute. She did not trust anyone. The continuing search for the son she put up for adoption had matured her well beyond her twenty-three years. Her parents asking for her forgive- ness was the only positive outcome from Dawn's search. They had treated her as a pariah when they learned she was pregnant. Now they were assisting her in finding more information about their grandson. She was still employed at Stones Uncovered. Dawn wondered why she didn't have a social life, maybe watching Mahogany's son made her feel closer to the son she didn't have. It was partially true. When Dawn held Lucas, the hole in her heart did get a little smaller.

*　　　*　　　*

Shanice removed her shoes and returned to the living room. She sat in a familiar spot on her brown leather couch and exhaled a deep breath. The words "almost there" kept running through her mind. She desperately wanted her marriage to be as it was before the separation, yet the closer she thought they were, the further the goal seemed. After having an affair, Shanice craved for a drastic a change in her life. Looking back, it was sad that she allowed a person other than her husband to fulfill her needs. It was an obvious fact that Omar neglected Shanice emotionally and physically, but she now realized that his actions did not give her a "free cheat" card. Things were different now, Omar made an effort to be more attentive and that was enough for her. She chose to make an effort as well to keep her family together. It was a payoff that she wasn't willing to take a chance on.

"Babe, I really appreciate you changing your plans. Something unexpected came up." Omar rubbed her lower back consolingly, "Do you need me to bring you anything back?"

"No, not at all," murmured Shanice.

This was becoming a habit. Omar would leave and be gone for hours. Although, when she call his cell phone he was always available. It seemed he wanted to keep her at home and not allow her to have a life outside of him. Shanice was willing to do whatever it took to regain Omar's trust. When they decided to reconcile, he didn't exactly welcome her with open arms. Yet he relented for the sake of Chloe. Deep down she believed that Omar would not have been so angry if the affair had been with a man. She crushed his ego by cheating with a woman. Now, a couple of years later, she managed to fix the relationship she tore apart and it would stay that way as long as she could control it.

*   *   *

Tonight Mahogany promised her friend, Joshua, that she would join him at his church, Calvary Fellowship, and check out the scene. As she drove to the church, she hoped the visit would relieve some of her mental stress. Mahogany left details with Dawn on where she could be reached. They agreed to meet in the foyer of the church. He was the instructor at her trauma group meetings. They managed to keep in touch after her sessions were completed.

Joshua Neumann stood a foot over everyone in the lobby. His long dreads cradled the strong features of his face. His piercing brown eyes and cleft chin gave him an aura of mystique. There was no way a person could tell that he was Jewish simply by looking at him. He reminded Mahogany of Tupac Shakur because of the strong passion he had for life. It comforted her to see how excited he was for his church.

"Mahogany, it's great to see you," he hugged her.

"Same to you, Joshua," Mahogany looked around, "You're not late at all."

"No, I thought I would be. Where is your friend?" inquired Joshua. "She couldn't make it."

"That's too bad. I hope everything is okay," he seemed generously concerned. The loud choir music could be heard through the foyer, "Let's go take a seat before service starts," he recommended. Mahogany followed him as he led the way inside the church. A lush burgundy carpet was lined wall to wall throughout the building. Dark brown colored pews were situated in a huge octagon shape around the pulpit.

They immediately took their seats. Mahogany leaned towards Joshua to ask him the name of the speaker, but he was already enthralled with the sermon. The pastor of the church had asked the congregation if anyone wished to share their testimony before church and a middle aged woman stood up. The pastor immediately recognized her.

"Sister Watson, please tell us how the Lord blessed you."

"Pastor Ethan, this past weekend I attempted to take my life." The room instantly grew quiet. "I swallowed a whole bottle of sleeping pills. I believed that all my problems were going to be solved by those pills and when I awoke, I was in a very dark place." Her voice never cracked. It was steadfast in her delivery.

"It was cold and I have never felt so alone in my life. There were deep shadows that surrounded me. I could never see a face. Each time I tried to see who or what it was, a strong fear would grab my heart, stopping me from speaking." Her voice dropped an octave.

"I began to cry, wishing that I wasn't there anymore, and how I did not want to die. Then one of the shadows jumped onto me, covering my chest so I couldn't breathe I managed to say 'Jesus' and then I woke up. "Jesus" that was it. All I know is that the place I went to was not Heaven and I need you to tell me how to get there."

She sat back down and all eyes watched as tears silently fell down her cheeks.

Pastor Ethan closed his Bible and asked Sister Watson to come to the front of the church.

"Do you believe Jesus Christ is the Son of God and that he died for your sins?" he asked.

"I do," she whispered.

"Then you must believe in your heart, mind, and soul in the salvation of Christ and you will be saved."

Pastor continued, "If there is anyone unsure of where they will be when they die, please come to the front of the church. Don't waste time, Sister Watson was blessed that she called out to the Heavenly Father and he rescued her. Someone out there may not be so lucky, why take a take a chance on your life?"

Mahogany observed few people rise out of their seats, willing to start a new beginning. She didn't need Pastor Ethan's advice. She had been taught the ways of the Lord, inside out. Her mother had held Bible study every Friday night and her family attended church every Sunday. "How many are sure as to where you are going?" he echoed. Mahogany remained in her seat. She was positive about her final destination.

After arriving home, Mahogany told Dawn the events of the night. "I'm just so happy that I'm saved," Mahogany sighed.

"What is that supposed to mean?" snapped Dawn.

"It just means that I'm saved that I won't end up where that old lady did."

"Oh, Mahogany, what are you talking about? Do you hear yourself? I don't believe in your quote unquote Jesus. Does that mean I'm going to hell? I'm already booked on a one-way ticket to hell, right?"

Dawn heard the same crap from her parents. The same parents who forced her to give her son up for adoption and if her own parents who had Jesus caused her unbearable pain, what does that say about all the other so-called Christians? They were people who proclaimed one thing and did another. Religion wasn't a subject that she and Mahogany discussed much, but tonight Mahogany hit a button with her righteous claim to salvation. Not to mention, Mahogany seemed very condensing in her attitude, acting like she was better than everyone who didn't agree with her beliefs. Mahogany's mouth hung agape after Dawn's tirade.

"You know that is not what I meant, Dawn. What is going on with you? I say one thing and you want to jump all down my throat? And it wasn't even directed toward you."

"Listen, I understand all that, but you remind me of the hypocrisy of my parents."

"Okay, with all due respect, I'm not your parents."

Mahogany was still smarting from Dawn's rant against her. "Also, it seems that you have way too much anger towards your parents. You need to resolve those issues, whatever they may be or it will eat you up on the inside like a cancer."

That was the last straw. Dawn had enough of Mahogany and her mouth.

"Just answer me this: how do you know that you are right? That your belief is the only correct belief? Because your mom told you and her mom told her and so on? Does anyone in your family think for themselves?"

"Of course they do," answered Mahogany. "I have decided that they are right and everyone else is wrong."

"I see, because some imaginative guys a book over two thousand years ago called the Bible, right?"

Mahogany did not have a response for her. The words spoken by Dawn were true. She was raised in the church and that was all that she knew, she did not see any reason to question the information. It was like if her mom told her the sky was blue, Mahogany didn't see any reason to ask why or how the sky was blue. It just was. Her mother was extremely definitive when it came to explaining life or death:

"You are going to live—no question about it. You are going to die—no question about it. Are you going to live after you die? Only God knows."

"I'll see to you later, Mahogany. Lucas had a good night, all he wanted to do was watch Barney and eat applesauce."

Dawn gathered her belongings and left. After locking up, she realized that Dawn did have a point. Mahogany could not argue much if she did not have evidence or proof to offer on what she believed to be true. She would find the evidence to support her beliefs and settle it. After all, how hard could it be?

*   *   *

Omar sat at his desk typing furiously on the computer. The walls of his office were decorated with various achievement awards, but his most important achievement was in a wooden frame located on the corner of his desk. It was a picture of him with his family. He took a moment to outline his wife's face with the tip of his finger. He hoped that he truly had her heart—for good this time. He had thought so before, but unfortunately that was not the case. He and Shanice had regrettably chose the option to hurt one another. He recently received a promotion to editorial assistant of the North Carolina Post. With his new position came new responsibilities. The upcoming deadline that drew him away from home involved covering the story on who would be the next Pope. Who cared about the new Pope? Evidently the majority of their readers, the Carolina Post recently held a contest asking who would be appointed and they had received over ten thousand responses from the readers. Cardinal David Ibraham seemed to be the leading contender. People had too much time on their hands, but that was fine. People like that helped write his paycheck. His cell phone rang.

Shanice's voice came through, "Hey babe, I just wanted to ask you to pick me up something from the grocery store on your way back."

"I don't know how long I'm going to be here. What did you need?"

"Some Breyer's Vanilla Ice Cream, I'm making a peach cobbler. I think it's someone's favorite." A big grin broke out on Omar's face. She knew just what to say to make him smile.

"Hmmm, I can bring it in a little over an hour. I have to write a column on David Ibraham, he's giving a speech. Have you seen anything on the television?"

"Yes, a couple of media outlets showed him speaking in front of his house in Jordan. Sorry, I forgot the name of the town he was in."

Omar could understand how she forgot the name. He had a hard enough time pronouncing different Middle Eastern names.

"That's fine. I'll turn on the TV here and see what they're saying. Let me go, so I can get home quicker and get some of that cobbler. My mouth is watering already."

"Alright, I'll put it in the oven now, so when you get here it will be piping hot. Talk to you later. I love you."

"Love you too."

He had to give her credit for trying to turn their marriage around and it was working. He was happy with his life. He had a wife who loved him and a daughter that he worshipped the ground she walked on. In the beginning of his marriage he was distant and did not particularly care about the feelings of his wife. Omar chose to do whatever he wanted, so he took some of the blame for his marriage almost failing. However, it still hurt that Shanice left him. When she admitted to cheating on him, let alone with another woman, he didn't know how to handle it. But when she came to him asking for another try, he didn't see the harm. At first, he had intentions to get even with her but, when 9/11 happened, everything was put into a different perspective. He only had one family and life was too short to focus on the negative. The terror attacks showed that tomorrow was not guaranteed to anyone. The United States had captured Saddam Hussein, world leaders were speaking of finally achieving peace in the Middle East, and in all honesty, the world seemed safer. Shanice deserved credit for putting her best back into the marriage. She caused him fall in love with her all over again. His cell phone rang again, by the caller-ID he could tell that it was Shanice.

"If you keep calling me, I'll never get finished in time for the cobbler," he started.

"Are you watching the news?" She sounded panicked.

"No, I haven't turned the TV on yet, why?" He rushed to find the remote for the television in his office.

"Someone just tried to assassinate David Ibraham."

Omar turned on the television to see what seemed to be left of David Ibraham's house. Bellows of smoke were cascading from the windows. He turned up the volume so he could hear the reporter,

"Minutes ago, Mr. Ibraham was taken to the Abdullah Hospital by the Jordanian ambulance. Ambulance officials report that Mr. Ibraham is suffering from minor burns and abrasions on both arms. Many are saying it's a miracle that he escaped alive."

Omar listened to the reporter ramble on, but all he could think about was how Ibraham's assassination attempt would dramatically influence the world and how busy he would be for the next couple of days. There was no doubt that Mr. Exum, his supervisor, was going to make him work double, maybe even triple time to see who or what was behind the assassination attempt. After all, nothing sells newspapers like a great story. He regrettably told Shanice he would be home in a few hours.

*   *   *

Damien closed his eyes from the stress. He either was on the verge of making the company an immense amount of money or helping the company lose millions of dollars if he didn't play his cards right. He received an insider tip on a business that was going to change the world in a major way. Having worked for Phoenix Technology a little over seven years, he had yet to receive his due. Damien understood that his big break may have finally arrived.

The name of the company was Digital Connections. According to his source, the CEO of Digital Connections would be terminated before the day ended. Damien had to convince Michael Reed that his idea was a once in a lifetime opportunity for Phoenix Technology.

"Mr. Andrews, they're ready to see you now," said Mr. Reed's secretary.

She ushered Damien into a roomy office that was obviously showered in expensive European decor. Mr. Reed was seated behind his black oak Chippendale desk while the C.F.O., Bart Wendell sat on a white suede couch near the corner window sipping what looked like a rum and coke.

"Hello, Damien. Good to see you."

Michael stood up to shake his hand. His handshake was indicative of how he did business, very firm and quick. He was an older gentleman in his late fifties. Always wore a suit and tie, he was never late. Everyone that ever did business with Michael thought they walked away with a great deal—an illusion that many seemed to buy. His only flaw was a ridiculous four strand comb-over that he refused to let go.

"I trust that you haven't been waiting too long," Michael continued. "No, not at all," said Damien.

"Please have a seat. Bart is going to be joining us. I hope that's not a problem."

Bart Wendell had fiery-red hair that matched his tenacity to "shoot and fire." Shooting off at the mouth and firing people at the drop of a dime were Bart's signature moves. Nope, it wasn't a problem at all. Sitting down in the chair across from Michael, Damien began his presentation.

"Okay gentleman, I'll get straight to the point. We need to buy out Digital Connections or at the very least invest fifty percent of our assets into this company by this Friday."

Damien could tell from their blank stares his suggestion was not something that piqued their interest. He hurriedly continued.

"As you both know, Digital Connections has been on the cutting edge of technology. You may recall reading stories on their ability to develop an injectable microchip implant for humans. The…"

"Why would we invest in that company?" Bart interjected. "Digital Connections has been having difficulties all year?"

Damien answered quickly. He prepared himself for their questions. "Yes, they have. Their main problem was getting an approval from the FHA to use their product. There was some concern about the side effects on humans. However, Digital Connections proved that the subdermal Radio Frequency Identification Data chip, otherwise known as R.F.I.D., is basically the same thing that has been used in pets for the past ten years. The FHA has since reversed its decision and all systems are a go for marketing to the masses."

"I still fail to see the relevance of the reversed FHA decision and Phoenix Technology's need to quickly purchase or invest in the company," Bart remarked. He required more pros than cons before he even thought of signing off a big deal such as this.

"Well, I received an insider tip about the CEO of Digital Connections. He will be fired today. It seems this C.E.O., Carl Wilder was the main obstacle between a merger of Digital Connections and all the major credit card companies."

Damien smelled victory entering the room. Gone were the blank stares, he saw curiosity lurking in their eyes. Damien fought back a smile as he continued.

"Wilder wanted the R.F.I.D.'s to be mainly used as GPS tracking devices. He saw the potential for people to get "chipped" out of fear for their children being kidnapped or families "chipping" members who had Alzheimer's that may get lost. Worried family members could easily find them. The chip emits a radio-frequency signal to the GPS satellite transmitting the person's location. Where Wilder messed up was trying to keep the R.F.I.D.'s solely for GPS purposes. So the board members terminated him for hindering the company. Not only will the new focus of Digital Connections include a GPS tracking system, but will also include a fraud-proof design payment method for cash and credit-card transactions."

Damien saw Bart and Michael eyes start to gleam at the new prospect. He handed them the charts and graphs detailing his next points.

"According to Federal Trade Commission estimates, identity fraud cost the banking industry forty-eight billion dollars a year, and consumers five billion. We're talking about billions of dollars. People have been paying with A.T.M., debit, and credit cards, which helped the world become a very cashless society. I submit to you, gentlemen that Digital Connections sub-dermal implants will one day emerge as the ultimate solution for a world fraught with identity theft from criminals to terrorist. It's time for us to act."

Michael spoke for the first time as he looked over the documents. "I'm sold. Bart, how soon can we draw up the contracts?"

"It won't take very long to implement. My only concern is the privacy advocates. They will argue that other companies will have access to their personal information and that is something Digital Connections cannot control. The gathering of the information and who will have access to it."

"Not to worry," reassured Damien. "Digital Connections will house the main database where all information is gathered. In addition to the sub-dermal chip, they will manufacture hand-held and portal readers that will scan the data when an employee enters a building, room, hospital, or makes a payment in a grocery store."

"It seems you have thought of everything, Damien," Bart grinned. "This venture seems to be a win-win situation. How can we lose by saving billions of dollars that are used to fight identity theft?" he questioned.

"We rarely agree on anything, Bart, so this must be a good decision or pigs must be flying," laughed Michael. "Damien, I want you to excuse us. We have a pressing appointment, but your idea looks like a good one. I want you in the meeting with the Board of Directors just in case they want to play hardball."

"Thank you for your time gentlemen, I look forward to embarking on this new mission," finished Damien.

After leaving the office, Damien wanted to tell someone—any- one—about how great the meeting went. The only person who came to mind was Mahogany. Her name was still etched across his heart, no matter what he did to try to erase it. She will always have a piece of him, though he made it hard for her to believe so. Their relationship was a bit tenuous after the birth of Lucas. Damien tried to be there for her and his son, but something always got in the way. It was selfish of him to realistically expect that after cheating on Mahogany, she would instantly trust him for the sake of their son. Her lack of trust and the stress of her unwarranted accusations took a toll on their relationship that could not be replenished.

Mahogany was a fantastic woman. He could not have asked for a better mother for his son. If only he could turn back the hands of time, he would erase his foolish actions. Currently, he wasn't dating anyone. The opportunity was there, yet, he just didn't have any interest in the courting game. It was ironic. Playing the "game" is what made Damien pay the ultimate price. Damien lost the one person who truly loved him. He didn't know how to describe it, but he sensed a change within Mahogany when it came to him. No longer did she care how many women called his cell phone. The only thing that mattered to Mahogany was making sure he was there for his son, Lucas. That was the beginning and the end of their relationship. It was three years ago when he first spotted her in the elevator. She worked as an intern. Her eyes were so full of life and lit up when she looked at him. Damien snuffed his light out when he became unfaithful. Would she ever look at him in that way again? Grabbing his cell phone, he dialed Mahogany's number.

"Mahogany, you will not believe what happened today."

*   *   *

Omar flipped through his rolodex. International newspapers buried his desk. His sources were tapped out. Two days had passed since the attempt on Ibraham's life. He pooled through his sources to see if any leads would turn up. The media confirmed through unnamed sources that the rogue Arab militia group Hamas was responsible. But why? Another strange piece of the puzzle was the three suicide bombings in Israel timed simultaneously with the Ibraham's assassination attempt. The article he wrote for the Carolina Post yesterday detailed the usual unrest that followed in the Middle East whenever potential peace was on the horizon. The attack on Ibraham should have been foreseen or even prevented by the United Nations or the Jordanian police. Israel and the rest the world had been in shambles. Omar didn't know how it all connected. He remembered the headlines years ago: "Yasser Arafat Rejects Rare Peace Offer!"

Ehud Barak, the former Prime Minister of Israel, offered Arafat, the head representative of the Palestinians, everything he wanted on a silver plate: including control over the disputed territories in the West Bank and Gaza Strip. Palestinian prisoners who had been convicted of committing terrorist acts against the Jewish state were pledged freedom. Jewish communities on historically Jewish lands would be dismantled. And the biggest olive branch of them all: offering to divide the sacred capital city, Jerusalem, with the Arabs. Barak went on record saying, "Arafat is liar. In the Arab culture, it is accepted, a time-honored tradition to lie and break treaties to non-Muslims. It's part of their Koranic law called the *Hudaibiya*. Treaties and contracts with people like Arafat are worthless." Omar did not understand the two thousand year old hatred between the Jews and the Palestinians. Their hatred spanned thousands of years and for what? A piece of land? It was too complicated of an issue for him to understand. He just wanted to write articles that sold papers and at the moment, his sympathetic position towards the women and children getting blown up by terrorist sold thousands of issues. Many did not see the difference between the 9/11 attacks and the suicide bombings taking place in Israel. Both circumstances contained people who were fighting for a "cause."

Mr. Exum poked his head in Omar's office. During the two years he worked for him, Omar never got tired of being around him. Although Mr. Exum made him work slave hours, Omar still had respect for him. He was the only person that Omar ever worked for that remembered his and every member of his family's birthday—plus his wedding. Mr. Exum was a rare jewel that still found a way to remain priceless in this day and age.

"How are we coming along with the Ibraham story? Any tips?" His eyes waited patiently for Omar's response.

"Mr. Exum…"

"Now, Omar, how many times do I have to tell you to call me Rodney?"

It didn't matter how many times he reminded him, Omar still did not feel comfortable calling him by his first name.

"Rodney, I've been touching base with my contacts at Langley and the White House, and they all say the same thing as everyone else. Hamas is responsible," replied Omar. The funny thing is that Israel claims that Hamas is denying they had anything to do with the assassination attempt."

"Who do we believe? Do we know why Hamas would do such a thing? I mean, this David Ibraham is a Muslim and wasn't he born in the Gaza Strip?"

"Indeed, he was. There must be something that we are overlooking," remarked Omar.

Omar did not have time to finish his sentence before a loud bang permeated through the office building. It was gunfire. The sound of glass shattering deafened his ears. Mr. Exum hit the floor scrambling to get near Omar's desk. Omar slowly rose from his seat and walked towards his door. He peeked outside to see what was going on. His office was situated in the back of the building near the boardroom. He would have to make his way around the corner to view the main lobby area. As he started down the hallway, a thunderous voice froze him in his tracks.

"I come to bring the wrath of vengeance and honor to my brothers' name! Where is Mr. Omar Miller?"

*   *   *

Mahogany sat at Chanell's, the local internet café, waiting for Joshua. Chanell's was located in downtown Raleigh. The building had been around for over thirty years and was within walking distance of North Carolina State University, which made it very popular for college students. The smell of fresh baked apple pie from the kitchen allowed many to feel that Chanell's was home away from home. Their state-of-the-art computers didn't hurt matters either. The small family owned business was an irreplaceable asset to the community. Gazing out a window, she witnessed the most beautiful sunset across the sky.

She had a five-thirty appointment. Today was the only free day in Joshua's calendar and Mahogany was on a mission to prove something to Dawn or maybe herself. Joshua had a wealth of knowledge concerning the bible and history, and Mahogany needed to speak with him before beginning her quest. The research was something she felt she could do in her spare time and there was no time like the present. Her spat with Dawn made her reevaluate and wonder why she believed in her faith, something which has sustained her through some very perilous times in her life. If Dawn caused her to doubt herself, what did that say about her belief system? She sipped on her white chocolate mocha latte and relished the sweet taste in her mouth. Why couldn't life be this sweet she thought? Joshua arrived at the café wearing khakis shorts and a white T-shirt. He stopped at the counter to place an order for large Chai Iced Tea.

"I like your work outfit," commented Mahogany on his casual attire. Joshua emitted a chuckle.

"I went home to change my clothes, I hope you don't mind. I won't ruin your glamour girl image with the public will I?" he joked.

Although she was joking with him, she could not help but admire his features. It wasn't that he was drop dead gorgeous. It was the manner in which he carried himself. Every ounce of his being oozed manliness. He wasn't cocky with it, it just was part of him and she found that attractive.

"No, not at all, thank you for joining me, I know you're a very busy man."

"I trust everything is okay. Are you still having nightmares?"

"I am. However, that is not why I asked you to meet me," stated Mahogany. "I need to pick your brain, why do you personally believe in Jesus? I had an argument with Dawn, she jumped down my throat for not being able to offer and explain why I believe what I believe. It's hard for me to explain, so I figured I'd ask for your opinion."

Joshua leaned back in his chair. The question posed by Mahogany caused a rainbow of emotions for Joshua, especially concerning his family. His parents finally started speaking to him. He looked forward to Yom Kippur approaching. One of its requirements was not to take excess baggage into the New Year. Joshua felt hurt by his parents' cold treatment. However, it was a minor punishment compared to his greater reward.

"Well," Joshua began. "It has been a long hard journey, mainly because I'm Jewish and for me to believe in this "Yeshua," as my father would say, is unheard of within the Jewish community. You know that the majority of my people are still awaiting their Messiah."

"Yes, that is why I'm asking you these questions. What was the turning point for you?" asked Mahogany.

Joshua held up two fingers and said, "Two things: Isaiah 53. Are you familiar with Isaiah?"

"I know that he was a prophet and God mainly sent him to warn Judah, the southern kingdom of Israel of God's impending judgment." Mahogany owed that tidbit of information to her Sunday school classes. She could tell that Joshua was impressed.

"You are correct, madam," he drank some of his tea and continued. "Now the Old Testament has over three hundred prophecies regarding the arrival of the Messiah. The book of Isaiah contributes to a number of them, the odds that one person could fulfill even ten of them is a statistical phenomenon. And Chapter Fifty-Three was the clincher for me."

"What did it say?"

Mahogany's interest was genuinely piqued. She brought her Bible and a notepad for their discussion.

His voice got louder with excitement, "Well, Isaiah begins by asking the Lord who has believed their report regarding the Messiah. He goes on to describe a man that is despised and rejected by men—a man that was wounded for our transgressions, and bruised for our iniquities. Yet, by this same man's stripes, we are healed. Isaiah even went so far as to detail how this man would die with the wicked but will lay with the rich upon his death."

His deep voice paused as he awaited her reaction.

"Hmm, Jesus dying on the cross with the criminals and being buried in a rich man's grave?" she asked. "I never knew that story was detailed in Isaiah."

Mahogany took notes of every word that Joshua spoke. She wondered why interesting subjects such as these were not mentioned in her church as she was growing up. It surely would have made the learning a lot more fun.

"Isaiah saw that the Messiah would willingly suffer for the sins of humanity by bringing justice, righteousness, and redemption to a sinful world," concluded Joshua.

"Were other prophecies mentioned?"

"In chapter seven, Isaiah tells the King of Judah that the Lord will give a sign: a virgin conceiving and bearing a son called Immanuel."

"Joshua, after you gave your parents this information, they still did not believe you?"

"No, not for a second, like the verse says, 'Who will believe our report?' but that is okay, I continue to pray for them. What more can I do, it's out of my hands."

Mahogany understood his position. Dawn sounded like a carbon copy of Joshua's parents. Mahogany could not convey in words to Dawn why she felt the way she did, but she was going to explain to her in detail why she believed in what she did.

Looking into Joshua dark eyes, she inquired, "Anything else factor into your transformation? What do you say to people who question the validity of the Bible?"

"I don't have anything to say to some people. The Bible is the only book on the earth has the ability to foresee events before they happen. We're talking thousands of years before they happened."

"You're talking about the birth of Christ?"

"No, I'm talking about the birth of the state of Israel." He saw Mahogany writing feverishly. "There's no need to write this down. It's already written down in the Good Book."

"Where is it at?" She was already flipping the pages. "I thought Israel had always been a state." He grabbed her fingers to stop the flying pages.

"I need your full attention in order for you to fully grasp what I'm about to tell you. How familiar are you with history?"

"Not very, well maybe a little familiar," she hedged.

Joshua excused himself from the table to order more coffee. After taking a deep gulp, he picked up where he left off. "Two thousand years ago, the people Israel were uprooted from their national homeland and were scattered to the four corners of the earth. In 70 AD, the Roman conquest of Israel marked the end of the historic possession of Israel by the Jewish people. From 70 AD to May 14, 1948, the Jewish people never had a place where they could authoritatively call home. Keep in mind that the Romans changed the name of ancient Israel to 'Palestine' in an effort to erase the name of Israel from the pages of history. And so it is from the Roman's the association of the word "Palestine" became connected to Israel, not because Arabs from surrounding countries moved to Israel and began to call themselves Palestinian. Even though Rome attempted to stamp out the name of Israel from the world's memory, God had promised to reassemble the Jewish people back to their homeland, and the twentieth century personally witnessed God honoring His promise with the Jewish people."

"Where is that promise written?" asked Mahogany.

"The book of Ezekiel, chapter eleven verse seventeen and do read Isaiah, chapter sixty six verse eight. Nothing like knowing you are living in a modern day miracle, right?"

"Yea," she responded pensively, "Nothing like it."

*   *   *

Mr. Exum made it safely underneath Omar's desk, skewing the eye glasses on his face. He wondered what happened to security and how a lunatic would be able to enter the premises with a gun. The first thing he would do if he made it out alive would be to sue the security company for mental duress. Omar must have thought that he was captain save-a-co-worker by going directly into the fray. There was gunfire everywhere and unless someone offered him a million dollars, Mr. Exum was not moving. His mama didn't raise a fool. He heard footsteps shuffling around in the office. Peering from his position he could tell the shoes were Omar's.

"Omar," Mr. Exum whispered. "What did you see out there?"

"I couldn't see anything, but I heard plenty." Omar stooped near the floor and grabbed the phone off his desk and dialed 911.

"My name is Omar Miller, I work at the Carolina Post and there is a raging gunman in our office." Omar heard the yelling get louder and louder near his office. "No I did not see him, but I heard him and he is mighty pissed off at someone. He said something about bringing vengeance and honor to his brothers. No, I don't know if there is more than one person or not."

"Listen, I can't stay on the phone long. He is right outside my door," he told the operator. Omar placed the phone down and scooted underneath his desk beside Mr. Exum. The door slowly creaked opened and a barrage of bullets quickly followed suit.

"Come out Mr. Omar Miller. Don't tell me that you are cowering in your luxury hideout, hiding from me. I've always suspected that you were a man who would cringe at his own shadow."

The gunman, Ali Zoudeide, knew directly where Omar's office was located. He saw him enter it every day.

Ali had spoken to his brother in the Persian Gulf the night before and the news from home was troubling. The rumors were true. The Americans were officially launching a Christian holy war against Islam. The war in Iraq was just the beginning of their onslaught. The Koran had warned of the infidels, who would fight them until his brothers abandoned their religion. That would never happen. Ali had paid close attention to the articles written by Omar over the years—articles that called for penalties against his Palestinian brothers who continued to destroy the Zionist-Israel. Everyone back home knew that Muslims were facing a new crusade bought by the Jews and the Christians. All someone had to do was listen to the President of the United States, Roy Dean Williams, he declared that America's war against terrorism was a war in the name of God; even adding that God had chosen the American people to fight such a war. Ali believed the war won in Iraq would ricochet in America and the Muslims in the United States would soon be in danger and should prepare themselves for a battle against the American people. Ali decided that today was the day he would rage his battle in opposition to the man that fed the hungry appetites of the pigs who wished to harm his fellow countrymen.

Omar debated on coming out from underneath his desk, Mr. Exum had a grip on his arm that almost stopped the blood circulation. However, the decision was not one he could control: Omar's cell phone rang.

"Come out now with your hands up!" Ali demanded.

Omar and Mr. Exum followed his instructions, both men recognized Ali immediately. He worked in the janitorial department and kept to himself. He was always absent from company functions. Omar's phone continued to ring.

"Mr. Miller hand me your telephone," ordered Ali. Omar did as he was told.

"Ali, what are you doing?" inquired Omar.

Mr. Exum stood in silence. He could not believe his ears or his eyes. Standing before him was a man he helped personally hire and standing next to him was a man bold enough to ask questions to a man pointing a gun at him. Mr. Exum decided that he was not going to question anyone, not to speak to unless spoken to first, nor make direct eye contact.

"Do not try to solicit information from me," Ali placed the phone in his pocket. "Both of you go into the board room, and hurry up."

As he exited the room, Omar noticed that the lobby was empty, he hoped some of his co-workers managed to escape. Upon entering the boardroom he saw that few did, there were about thirty people huddled in a corner.

Omar began, "Ali, what is all this about? You don't want to do whatever this is. If this is about me, please let these people go. Having them here is not going to accomplish anything. Think about it."

"Shut up!" Ali shoved both men further into the room and locked the door. "I'll tell you what this is all about. It's about you using this newspaper as a bludgeon against my brothers." Omar had no idea what Ali was referring to. "Mr. Miller, you heralded the U.S. forces triumph over my country men in Iraq. These same U.S. forces you want to bestow congratulatory medals on have murdered and maimed many women and children in the name of 'war.' Then you, a citizen of America wonders why there is a hatred for this forsaken country."

Omar was taken aback by Ali's rage and resentment. He thought the best thing for him to do was to keep Ali talking in order to keep Ali's mind off the gun.

"Okay, Ali, what is it that you want from me? To retract my stories, fine I will."

"No, Mr. Miller, I want your blood," Ali laughed ominously. "Think about it. What better way to give the media a lesson they will never forget? A lesson that will teach them they will pay a price with their life if they choose to write hateful propaganda for the United States

Government." Omar could hear his heart beating in his ears as Ali cradled the gun close to his chest.

"Think about what you are doing Ali. You seem to be a very intelligent man. What about the domino effect of your actions. Ten thousand more newspapers will write about you and how America needs to infiltrate other Islamic countries to make sure people like you stop getting brainwashed into believing that the United States is the great Satan."

"That's where you are wrong. 'People like me,' as you say, will pick up where I leave off because this is only the beginning." Omar watched in horror as Ali cocked the gun.

"Tell me, Ali, tell me. What did I do that is so wrong that you need to kill me? Sure, I've written articles about the United States victory in Iraq, so have many other journalists. Are you telling me that this is what your gun show is about? Your team lost and now you have to find someone and beat him up. If you asked me, that's a pretty sorry excuse to kill someone."

"Yesterday, Mr. Miller, what did you write about yesterday?" Ali coldly asked. Omar thought a moment. It was nearly impossible to think under such pressure.

"I wrote about David Ibrahim's assassination," he stammered, "and the homicide attacks' in Israel."

"Do you recall what you wrote about the suicide bombers of the terror attacks?" Omar remembered exactly what he had written down and he knew that Ali did too.

"I believe I wrote if suicide bombers thought that seventy-two virgins were waiting them in the afterlife then they were dumber than lambs lined up for slaughter."

The butt of Ali's gun hit Omar in the head, warm blood gushed down the side of his face.

"That was it," agreed Ali. "Those were your exact words!" His voice was near screaming. "I have no problem erasing you. You want to diminish the value we place in our religion by insulting the very tenants that we cherish. It's obvious!" Ali's breath was hot on Omar's cheek, as he began to whisper. "I know all about the evangelical agenda, an agenda that calls for the destruction of the Al Aqsa mosque in Jerusalem. We are aware of the Christian and Jewish alliance to fulfill the prophecy between the Nile and the Euphrates."

Omar had a hard problem concentrating on the conversation, the pain vibrated through his head. Mr. Exum thankfully had caught him before he hit the floor.

"Listen, Ali, I'm positive we have a misunderstanding here. I have no idea, virtually no idea what or who the Al Aqsa is."

"You do," Ali disputed. "Even if you don't know, you do, that's how it works. Yes, the conspiracy between Israel and the United States to take the mosque back has spanned for over fifty years. Maybe my actions here and in the present will do something for the future of tomorrow."

Omar could hear the resignation in Ali's voice and it terrified him. Not only that, the cold dark void in Ali's eyes complimented his jet black hair. The idea of not ever seeing Shanice or his daughter again scared him beyond belief. Omar believed in choices, everyone had a choice to make in life. People lived with choices whether they liked them or not. The funny thing about choice was that no one knew what another person would do if he or she was against a wall. Granted a person could pick and choose as much as he or she wants to. Yet the most significant thing about choice was to make a right one versus a wrong one. God help him! Omar lunged for the gun. He was about to make what he believed to be the right decision.

*　　　*　　　*

Joshua watched Mahogany scribble on her notepad. She had come a long way since their initial meeting. When they first met, she was a frightened woman who seemed to have no sense of direction as to where she wanted to go in life. She was pregnant and made it a point to keep to herself. In the counseling sessions, it took him months to wear down the barriers she put up. Not that he blamed her, she had good reason to put up a wall. Many of the men that she trusted had hurt her either emotionally or physically. He knew very little about Damien Andrews, but what he did know did not seem flattering. Mahogany shared with him stories of Damien's unfaithfulness and how in the past, she unwisely continued to be there for him no matter what he did to her. Now, when she mentioned Damien, it was only in the context of him being there for Lucas. Joshua wondered if there was something more Mahogany wasn't telling him regarding her relationship with Damien. He liked her and wanted to take their friendship to the next level, but he needed to move slowly so not to scare her away. When looking at her, all he wanted to do was hug her and tell her that everything would be okay. It seemed that no one had done that for her in a long time.

"How about we change the subject for a minute?" prompted Joshua. "Tell me about your nightmare."

"It was the same thing; you know the usual, Jake trying to kill me. But things were a little different," Mahogany looked away from Joshua. "We were kissing each other, Jake and I, very passionately and all of sudden I could not breathe. I would try to pull my face away to get some air but he is pinning me down with his body, I can't move, can't breathe. I start to blackout and then I wake up."

"That is a little different." Joshua guiltily glanced at Mahogany's lips.

"Why am I dreaming about making out with the guy that tried to murder me?" Mahogany's eyes welled with water.

"Well, don't forget you were forming a relationship with this person. It is quite normal," Joshua reasoned. He grabbed her hand in a show of comfort.

"These nightmares are not normal, Joshua. I want to move on with my life. These dreams are holding me in a pattern that I do not want to be in. What can I do?"

"The way I see it, you are still blaming yourself for what happened. Your dreams are an example of this. You need to think of defeating Jake. I know right now it seems rather difficult, but in your dreams when you are with Jake you need to overpower him and stop letting him control you. Replay what you will do over and over in your head until you manifest it into your dreams."

Mahogany knew he spoke the truth. She felt like an idiot for not being able to move on with her life. How many times had she seen people on those TV talk shows crying about something that happened years ago and thought they were just doing it for sympathy? Now look who was crying?

"Thank you for your advice, Joshua. Sometimes it's easier said than done."

"You're welcome. Now where did we leave off?" Mahogany looked through the pages of her notes. "You were discussing the rebirth of the state of Israel. How is that significant?"

"That I can't tell you," admitted Joshua. "I only know that it signifies the coming of the Lord."

"Explain," requested Mahogany.

"I'll try, but you really should speak to Pastor Ethan. He is the one who helped me find my way," he answered. "Pastor Ethan explained that with the birth of the state of Israel, the end-times clock began ticking."

"What do you mean?"

"He mentioned numerous things that would happen during the Last Days."

"Do you believe that we are living in the Last Days?" Mahogany deeply valued Joshua's opinion and wanted to know his position.

"Honestly, I don't know, because prophecy isn't my forte." He laughed. "But listen, Pastor Ethan is leaving town sometime this week and I don't know how long he's going to be away. If I were you, I would get up with him before he leaves."

"All right, I'll make an appointment." Mahogany put away her notepad and pen. "Tell me, what are your plans for this week?" A smirk appeared on Joshua's face.

"Why? Do you want to join me?" he pressed.

"No, I already have my work cut out for me with this little research project. I do want to thank you for meeting with me and answering a lot of personal questions. I know it wasn't easy. This thing with Dawn, it brought up a lot of questions that I should have already been asking myself." Mahogany looked at her watch and noticed she was running late on picking Lucas up from day-care. She planted a quick peck on Joshua's cheek.

"I'll be seeing you, Josh. I hate to run out on you, but I have to get Lucas. Touch base with me, okay." Mahogany's cell phone began to ring.

"Sure, maybe we can catch a sermon this Friday or something," Joshua mentioned. He watched her leave the coffee shop in a hurry. They would definitely meet up again soon.

Mahogany answered her cell phone near her car. "Hello?"

"Mahogany, this is Shanice. Have you seen the news?"

"No. I've been meeting with Joshua. Why? What's going on?"
Mahogany could hear the hysteria in her voice.

"There is a hostage situation down at the Carolina Post building and I
have been trying to call Omar on his cell but it just goes directly into his
voice mail. I can't get an answer. I know that he would answer if
everything was alright."

Mahogany spoke slowly in an effort to calm her down, "Shanice, did
you speak to Omar today?" Mahogany asked.

"Yes, earlier. A couple of times tonight."

"Listen, why don't we just go down to the Post building? I'll ask
Damien to pick Lucas up, okay?" "Good idea," reasoned Shanice.

"It will take me about ten minutes to get down there. What about you?"

"I can be there in five if I ignore the speed limit. I'll ask the neighbor's
to watch Chloe until we get back."

"Great! We'll go down there and you can see with your own eyes that
Omar is fine. Trust me. We'll meet in the lobby."

It wasn't like Shanice to over react unless she had good reason.
Mahogany hoped that Omar was fine. As she started the ignition of her
car, caravans of sirens swept pass the coffee shop parking lot. She
prayed that she was right.

*   *   *

There was chaos everywhere. Policemen ushered Mahogany's car pass
the office building. She saw yellow perimeter taped around the whole
structure. A large group of people stood outside, she could not see the
front of the building. A knot began to form in the pit of her stomach.
After parking her car, she rushed to the building. Her eyes busily
scanned for Shanice through the growing crowd. Television cameras and

news reporters were offering their own scenario of what was occurring inside the building to local viewers.

"Witnesses say two gunmen forced themselves inside, injuring the security officer."

"Reliable sources have told us that a disgruntled employee has vowed revenge on those responsible for the termination of his job."

"Local officials have confirmed that there are hostages inside. They have no idea what has set off the perpetrator. They do know that he is armed and dangerous. Police will have to wait and see what they can use as a bargaining chip in order to ensure that lives will not be lost."

Mahogany heard a familiar voice yelling within the crowd.

"My husband is in there. You don't understand I need to get in there!"

"Ma'am, I do understand that. My orders were to make sure no one was to get pass me. I'm sorry, but it's for your own safety."

Mahogany went to Shanice's side and placed her hand on her shoulder.

"My God, Mahogany," she whispered. "They won't let me go to him. I need to know what is going on."

"I know you want to, but you don't know what you would be walking into if the police allowed you to go in. They are only doing their job. Shanice, think for a moment, Omar would want you to be strong and not create a scene." Mahogany reassured her that Omar would be fine.

"You don't know that," accused Shanice. "I overheard one of his coworkers say that the gunmen asked specifically for Omar. Why would someone say that unless they meant him harm? I just want him here with me, right now. I don't want to ask anyone's permission to go see my husband." She pointed at her chest, "My husband, whose life may be in danger as we speak."

Shanice abruptly left. Mahogany watched from afar as Shanice continued to pace back and forth. She wished that she could say something to make her feel better. Glancing at the door entrance, Mahogany expected Omar to walk out with that devilish grin on his face. Both women continued to wait helplessly outside.

*   *   *

He had shot him. Ali was taken by surprise by Omar's attack. He tried to maneuver the gun towards Omar's body, but he lost his grip during the struggle and he had found himself on the opposite side of the gun barrel. Omar used his foot to throw Ali off balance and as Ali fought to regain his balance, Omar pulled the trigger. He had nothing to lose. When Ali slumped to the floor, Omar allowed the rage to pump through his body. He repeated kicked Ali in the head over the anger he felt towards him for trying to callously rob him of his life. Ali tried to rob his daughter of a father and his wife of a husband. Omar had never felt such raw emotion in all his life.

It was a low groan emitting from Ali's body that bought Omar back to reality. Mr. Exum placed his foot on Ali's neck.

"Give me a reason not to break it!" he demanded.

The hostages in the boardroom rushed to unlock the doors to freedom. Omar heard the S.W.A.T. team order everyone to stop in their tracks. It was over. Omar collapsed onto the carpeted floor. He couldn't stop his hands from shaking. He closed his eyes as the paramedic attended to his needs. What was this world coming to? A young EMT gentleman asked him several questions.

"Do you have any pain anywhere?"

"Just the gaping wound on my head," Omar answered.

"Well, I'm going to check your vital signs, okay? I need you to relax." While Omar followed the EMT directions, an older gentleman introduced himself.

"Mr. Miller, my name is Ed Snead. I work for the Department of Homeland Security. We need you to come down to the department in order for us to fill in some of the blanks and see if you recognize anyone that may belong to a terrorist cell that Ali could possibly be a part of."

"I know what cell he belonged to," offered Mr. Exum. "He was part of the crazy as hell cell! Don't know what's wrong with people today! How is he going to walk in here and just start shooting people? From now on, I'm working from home," he declared.

Walking on autopilot, Omar followed Mr. Snead through the lobby area. Even though a huge swarm gathered outside, the first person Omar laid eyes on was his wife. He stopped in his tracks when Shanice fell into his arms.

"What happened, baby? I've been so worried." She held Omar so tight he thought she would never let him go. Her arms made a vice grip around his waist.

"I'm fine, baby."

Omar explained the events of the day to her. Each tear drop that Shanice shed Omar kissed away. She could not comprehend the reason someone wanted to kill him no matter how many times he explained it to her. It was an incomprehensible action. Mr. Snead touched Omar's elbow, letting him know it was time to go. Omar introduced Mr. Snead to Shanice.

"I'm going to go with him to the Homeland Bureau and see if I can possibly help stop another nut from pulling off something like this," said Omar. He gave Shanice a reassuring hug.

"Good to meet you, Mrs. Miller. I wish it was under better circumstances," Mr. Snead grabbed Shanice's hand. "I promise to bring him back to you safely."

Omar had motioned for Mahogany to come over. She had stayed in the background, wishing not to interrupt Omar and Shanice. She wanted to give them what little privacy they could have.

"Mahogany, please, can you make sure she gets home safely," his eyes were red and tired. She wondered what he had been through today.

"Omar, you don't have to ask," replied Mahogany.

Omar kissed Shanice goodbye and went with Mr. Snead. He glanced back to blow her a kiss and mouthed, "I'll be home soon."

Shanice watched him leave with a heavy heart. Mahogany followed Shanice to her house and stayed with her for a couple of hours. She didn't know what to say. They had years of friendship but she thought silence was the best answer.

*   *   *

Omar opened the door to his house. He laid his jacket across the back of the sofa. The first thing that caught his eyes were the drawings his daughter made on the refrigerator. He walked into the kitchen and took a drawing from the fridge. His daughter claimed that it was a rainbow blanket that covered their house. He smiled thinking about what a real rainbow blanket would look like. A child's imagination was precious. It was a little past eight o'clock. He saw a little light coming out of Chloe's room and followed it. Before him was a sight that he would never forget as long as he lived. Shanice was seated on Chloe's bed reading a story to her, who was already fast asleep. Shanice glanced up from the book. She wore one of his old work shirts that was opened just right, and left very little to the imagination.

"Hey beautiful," Omar leaned over to kiss Chloe's forehead. He closed his eyes for a second, being grateful for his family. He slowly left the room before allowing his emotion to consume him. Shanice followed Omar out of the room.

"Did the bureau find out anything?"

"Yes and no," Omar reflected. "They went to Ali's apartment and found a lot of my articles in a shoebox and they are pretty positive he was an extremist. They just don't know if he was working for anyone, but from my conversation with Ali, I believe he was a solo act. You should have seen him. I've never seen such a deranged person." He quickly wiped his brow.

"Where is Ali now?"

"He's in critical condition at Wake General Hospital. They're waiting for him to regain consciousness. I almost killed him," confessed Omar.

"I'm sad that you didn't. Knowing that someone out there wants you dead is not a comforting thought."

Shanice walked to the refrigerator for a class of water. "He almost took you away from me?!"

Omar walked up behind her and began kissing the nape of her neck. "The only thing I saw was your face." He turned her around and kissed her gently on the lips. "When that gun was pointed at me, I didn't see my life flash before my eyes. I saw you, my life."

He kissed her very passionately and carried her into their bedroom to lay her upon the bed. He needed her comfort. Omar was a strong man but he needed the touch of his wife, the mother of his child, and his lover. He didn't know if it was because of his near death experience but he felt like this was the first time he was about to make love to her.

"I know that I put barriers between us trying to make you pay for something in the past. I apologize. I'm vowing to give you my all. If I leave this world tonight, I want you to know that I do love you."

"I am devoted to you, only you," she said softly.

Omar started at her feet. He wanted to treat her body like a creation made for his own necessities. Working his way up, he leisurely unbuttoned her shirt.

Shanice closed her eyes in arousal. It was a very emotional day for the both of them. She didn't know how to describe it, but there was a different vibe about him. He rose to remove his clothes.

"Don't move," he ordered in a voice hoarse from passion. His eyes drank up the body he yearned for. She looked so beautiful. Her dark brown hair was spread out against the pillow and she stared at him in a way he hadn't seen in a long time. His body responded accordingly.

"Is this real?" murmured Shanice, "Do you feel the same thing I do?" "I do. Trust me, I do," he grinned.

Returning to her side, he unhurriedly took off her shirt. He laid down beside her and ran his hand alongside her body, enjoying the soft feel of her skin. He wanted to relish this night along with her love. Taking hold of her face between his hands he kissed her passionately, avidly taking special care of her lips. Shanice responded in kind. He could feel her tears in the palm of his hands as he cradled her face.

"Don't cry," he begged.

"I can't help it. I realize what we have. I'll never take you for granted again. I'm sorry for hurting you, for the things that I did. I know I've told you this before, but I was selfish. I don't deserve you," she cried.

"Yes, you do. Stop beating yourself up, Shanice. You have made me fall in love with you all over again. I know that wasn't an easy thing to do.

Now I really need you to let me love you right now. I feel incomplete. I need you to make me feel whole again. I forgave you," Omar said.

Shanice pulled Omar over her, so that he completely covered her body. She released whatever guilt she was holding on to. It was an exhilarating feeling. A burden lifted from her shoulders and she finally felt free. Omar sensing that no longer did she hold back her emotions, kissed her.

Omar whispered in her ear. "I don't ever want to think about losing you."

"You won't have to," promised Shanice.

Omar took his time making love to her. Each time she touched him, he thought he would lose control. He swore their hearts were beating to the same tempo as their love making. He felt like he was dying all over again, except this time the deeper he went over the edge the more he wanted. He craved it. Shanice could tell by the tension of his shoulders that Omar was near losing control, they tightly contained the intensity of their passion. When he could not hold it in any longer, Shanice followed him and immediately climaxed. The room was deathly quiet. She finally had her family back.

Chapter Two

It was another dead end. Dawn bribed a lady who worked at an adoption agency in Boise, Idaho for the adoption papers on her son. It was the biggest lead she had in the last year. Boise was the origination point of where the adoption of Dawn's son took place. But the papers she received were falsified or the people giving the information lied. As she sat on the return flight to North Carolina, Dawn struggled not to give up hope. Maybe it was a sign, an unwelcome one, for her to give up the search. Yet, something kept driving her.

She wanted to see the son she was forced to give up with her own two eyes. Her parents were instrumental in her decision to give away her child. Dawn blamed them for her pain. She could never understand how they could do such a thing to their own flesh and blood. She carried anger towards them, but more so towards herself for not having the courage to stand up and say to them, "So, what if your grandchild is half-black, can't you love him still the same?" It was a scene that she replayed over and over inside of her head. When Dawn appeared on Mahogany's doorstep beaten to a pulp, she never believed a search for her son would soon ensue. She followed through on the promise she made to herself, by no means will she give up on her dream. Her son would turn six years old in four months.

The adoption form listed Lemar and Nina Fitzgerald as the adopters. However, there were no Fitzgerald's within a two hundred mile radius. To make matters even worse, no one had heard of Lemar or Nina. Dawn didn't understand. The information she purchased did not match up. People had to tell the truth on adoption forms and were put through a very stringent background check. If the information was correct, it meant that the Fitzgerald's had moved out of state, meaning Dawn hit another brick wall. She called Lieutenant Peck. He was her supervisor and the owner of Stones Uncovered.

"I know this is surprising," her voiced cracked, "but I hit another dead end."

"I'm sorry to hear that. I know your hopes were very high. I warned you of doing that," he cautioned. His boisterous voice boomed through the telephone.

Dawn appreciated Lt. Peck's honesty. His personality took some getting used to. Dawn knew that his grumpy disposition would transform into a gentle teddy bear. The words "crass" and "noisy" should have been his middle name. She assumed that made him a wonderful detective because of his raucous nature. Leave it to him to find a way to get paid for something he loved to do. People would never consider a man dressed as a field hand a threat. He familiarized himself with Dawn's search for her son and helped her by pulling information from all his resources. Adoption agencies were of a different feather, it was almost impossible to gather useful records from them.

"I know," she respected his honesty.

It was that same honesty that saved Mahogany's life. Lt. Peck solved the case when he realized that Jake was the psycho stalker terrorizing Mahogany. Everyone thought the stalker was Dawn's ex-boyfriend, Trent Royal. Trent was extremely possessive and abusive, he became hell bent on finding her after she left him. Dawn escaped and managed to move on without living in a world of fear thanks to Mahogany.

"I gave that woman a thousand dollars for bogus information," complained Dawn.

"You probably would have paid ten times that amount if she would have led you to your boy. Money isn't what this is about." Dawn reasoned his comments were correct.

"So what's my next move? I've covered all the bases. My parents gave me all the paper work they had. I just don't know where to go next."

"In this business, when it looks like you are looking for a needle in a haystack it's better to have someone get poked by the needle."

"What exactly does that mean?" Dawn asked.

"It means what it means. Sometimes you have to sit back and let the information come to you. Retrace your steps."

"Good idea, I have nothing else to do. I'll be in late tomorrow. My plane is landing at three in the morning."

"That's fine," he dryly replied. "We've managed without you before."

"Yes, I'm well aware of that. You have told me that a million times."

"Oh, before I forget, a Mr. Trent Royal called and left a number for you today. Any idea what he wants? I thought he was public enemy numero uno."

"I don't know what he could want," answered Dawn. Her mind returned to the years she lived under his abuse. "But I'm more than ready to find out," she declared.

*   *   *

Gabriel Kaufman reread the newspaper article one more time. It was his fourth time reading it. The headline read: *"The Western Wall is Weeping."* Tears gathered in his eyes. The article solidified what he already knew in his heart, his people were very close to rebuilding the House of the Lord. Gabriel continued to read aloud.

"Water has started to come out of the Western Wall. One of the stones, 15 meters up the wall, has suddenly become wet. Archeologist of the Israeli government assumed that the water might be coming from a broken pipe on the Temple Mount or from a water source that had been poured out close to the wall. However, the walls have thoroughly been checked and nothing was found to explain the presence of the water."

Gabriel's good friend, Steven Eisenberg, rushed into his office sporting a large grin. He was nearly out of breath from his sprint down the hallway. The moment he saw the article, he put on his shoes and made a bee line to their office.

"Gabe, have you seen the paper this morning?"

"Indeed I have," he responded. Gabriel's tanned skin was flushed with excitement.

It had been a long faithful struggle for both gentlemen. Gabriel founded the Shtiah Rock Assembly, a group devoted to the rebuilding the Third Temple upon the Temple Mount. It had been 1,934 years since the House of the Lord stood in the city of David and he believed it was his life's mission to rebuild it within his lifetime. The Al Aqsa Mosque sat on the exact location of the previous Jewish temples and Gabriel could not understand the complacency of his countrymen. Where was their furor to rebuild the Third Temple? Had they forgotten it? He devoted all of his time to rebuilding the temple.

"What day is in a little over a week?" questioned Gabriel. His eyes were bright from elation. Steven rubbed his bushy beard and looked at a wall calendar located by the bookshelf.

"It's Tisha B'Av," he yelled.

It was common knowledge that Tisha B'Av was a day that commemorated the destruction of both Jewish temples. Tradition held that the previous temples were destroyed on Tisha B'Av and the future Third Temple would be rebuilt on Tisha B'Av.

"Steven, there is no doubt that the water flowing from the Western Wall is a sign," Gabriel theorized. "Can you hear the footsteps of our Messiah, the Son of David? His arrival is near"

"What seemed impossible is now possible," rejoiced Steven.

The Israeli government was no doubt quaking in their boots, thought Gabriel. He was all too familiar with their shameful fear. The government wholeheartedly believed that the removal of the Al Aqsa mosque or even the mention of rebuilding the temple, would cause World War III. His leaders frustrated him with their lack of faith. He wished the government learned not to fear the world's reaction, but to only trust in the Lord. Yet, Israel always compromised her safety under the demand of the world. It was a spiritual weakness that may cost them their country. He was positive that once the rebuilding of the temple began, a positive change in the security, economic, and spiritual state of Israel would soon follow. Gabriel finished reading the last para- graph of the article:

"The prophet Ezekiel prophesied that water would flow from the Temple Mount during the Last Days which would be a sign of deliverance to the people and the land of Israel."

"You are correct, Steven," Gabriel agreed. "God has finally heard our cry."

Picking up the telephone, Gabriel called the one person in the world he knew that would be interested in the latest news on the Third Temple.

*   *   *

Damien went over the last details of the contract with Nicole. She was Mr. Reed's right hand and helped tie up the loose ends with Digital Connections.

"Damien, I see that you have thought of everything. Mr. Reed did say that you were the real deal Holyfield." Her elegant hands flipped through the papers. "For the record, will Digital Connections R.F.I.D. have the capabilities to broadcast a signal?"

"The R.F.I.D. tags will contain a small chip and an antenna, usually coiled, to broadcast a signal. So the answer to your question is yes."

Her eyes held his for a moment too long causing them both to feel a bit uncomfortable. Nicole Hunt was an alum of Howard University. Her prowess in the boardroom permitted her to work up the corporate ladder the hard way. Although, she had a reputation of crushing anything that got in her way, Damien found her to be a very easy going woman. Affirmative action did not get her the job. She was quick to let anyone know it was her hard work and business acumen which earned her the position. The micro-braids that flowed down her back were flawless. She was an attractive woman in a "Mary-Ann" kind of way.

"I see. I simply wanted to double check. I guess that's why I get paid the big bucks right?" she smiled.

Damien sat directly across from her desk and from his vantage point he could see part of her dark red bra. He inferred that she knew it was showing.

"I would assume so," offered Damien.

"Looks like all systems are a go. Phoenix Technology shall acquire Digital Connections within the next couple of days," she closed the folder, "Enough about business tell me something about you."

"That depends on what you want to know," he smirked.

She rose from her desk and sat in the seat next to him in a recliner. Most of the people had already left for the day. They were the only people there. Her office was on the twentieth floor. The windows allowed her to view the State Capitol building downtown.

"Honestly, I don't know that much about you, except what I hear." By Damien's silence Nicole chose to continue. "I hear that you are dating someone that works here." She pretended that she didn't know the history between Damien and Mahogany. The history of their relation-ship was common knowledge within the Phoenix Technology office building.

"You know you can't believe everything that you hear. Why don't you tell me what you want to know instead of sharing office gossip?" he suggested.

"Are you seeing anyone?" she asked.

"Why? Are you interested," his tone automatically grew seductive. "I don't know."

She looked over his features, trying to read him. Most guys would have jumped at an opportunity to be with her. However, Damien seemed to be an enigma, a very tall and handsome enigma. "Why don't we go out for dinner tonight and see what happens. Agreed?"

"Agreed, want to shake on it?" Damien softly shook her hand. "Let's say we meet at Cinelli's at eight o'clock."

"Deal." Nicole slowly removed her hand and watched him leave. Damien stopped in the hallway, he felt conflicted. All he could think of was Mahogany. When he touched Nicole's hand, the only thing he thought was that her hand wasn't as soft as Mahogany's. Her scent wasn't the same as Mahogany's. Standing in the hall, he realized something that he must have known all along: He wanted Mahogany back in his life. When he called Mahogany after the meeting he had with Michael Reed and Bart Wendell, she truly was happy for him. She even went so far as to tell him that she was proud of him. He wished Mahogany could say those same words on the way he treated her. Retracing his steps, Damien decided to tell Nicole he needed to cancel their dinner plans.

"Don't worry, everything is on schedule. I just confirmed with him about the antennas."

Nicole's back was turned away from the door as she spoke on the telephone.

"Yes, yes," Nicole said tiredly. "Understand that Stor-Mart and Phoenix Technology are positioning themselves at the front of an inevitable, new technological revolution. The public will be hesitant at first. We'll get the customary cries from the A.C.L.U., but in the long run we will eventually achieve our mission. Every person will be injected with the

R.F.I.D. and have at least one to three R.F.I.D. products in every house in America. Damien handed us the golden hen and didn't even know it. The hard part has already been done: the preconditioning. People are already use to identifying themselves with numbers, social security numbers, driver's license numbers, and don't forget smart cards. Hold on a sec." Damien reentered her office.

"Eight o'clock sharp at Cinelli's. Don't keep me waiting. I know you like to put in the long hours," he teased.

"I'll be on time," Nicole promised.

He gave her a sly wink and left. What was she up to and who was on the other end of that phone call? It wouldn't hurt to find out. If someone was using him, he wanted to know why.

*   *   *

Dawn called Mahogany to inform her about Trent's mysterious phone call. It had been a couple of days since her and Mahogany spoken to each other.

"What do you think he wanted?" asked Mahogany.

"Your guess is as good as mine. All I know is that he better not come here starting any mess. I've grown out of the cage he once placed me in," declared Dawn. "You know, I didn't find out anything when I went back to Idaho."

"I'm sorry to hear that, I know you placed a lot of optimism on the lead you were given. What did you find out?"

"Zilch is what I found out. There was no trace of the adoptive parents. Lt. Peck suggested that I sit back and relax to see what comes next. But that is hard to do when you want something so bad. How can I do absolutely nothing?"

"I know something you can do." "What's that?"

"You can pray," suggested Mahogany. "A little praying never hurt anybody and it'll probably help more than all that footwork you are doing."

Mahogany's words stung. It had been a couple of days since their argument. Dawn marveled at Mahogany's constant need to shove religion down her throat. Not to mention, her throwing gasoline on the fire by adding that Dawn's "footwork" was all for naught because she hadn't prayed did not help the situation.

"What exactly are you saying?" questioned Dawn. "Are you saying because I haven't bothered to pray is the reason why I haven't found my son yet?"

"No, why are you so defensive? All I'm saying is that since Lt. Peck recommended that you do nothing, then you might as well pray. What's the harm in that?"

"There's no harm in it, I just don't like the way you said it. Like "praying" will do more than what I'm already doing. I'm the one who's going through old adoption applications, I'm the one calling and bribing people for information, and I'm the one who flew all the way back to Idaho just to see if anything came from a minuscule lead. I'm doing it, not you or your God!"

"I'm not arguing with you tonight. Just know that since our last disagreement you have made me think. You were right when you asked me why I believed in my religion. My beliefs were built on how I was raised. At first I simply wanted to prove you wrong, but as I began to research my faith, I also needed to find out if what you said was true."

"And what did you find out?"

"I found out that you were right. I would like to share with you all the surprising information that I have found out about my religious beliefs. It's really quite interesting."

"No thanks, but please feel free to pray for me though. Oh by the way, where is Damien?"

"I don't know," replied Mahogany. "What does that have to do with the conversation?"

"Nothing," Dawn said smugly. "Tell me, when is the last time you have been with him—intimately?"

She knew where Dawn's question was leading. Mahogany had confided in Dawn that she slept with Damien about six months ago. After he dropped Lucas off, they reminisced about old times and one thing led to another. Before Mahogany could stop it, clothes were flying off. Their lovemaking was hot and passionate. The only thing missing were the emotions she used to have for him. The feelings were gone. She wasn't in love with him.

Dawn continued, "Don't you think it's a bit hypocritical of you to tell me what I should be doing when I see you quote-unquote committing a sin? You? Mahogany Fox, the same person spewing this religious rhetoric?" Dawn knew she had her.

"Listen Dawn, if you don't want to hear it from me because of the issues you have with me then why don't you come with me tomorrow. I'm meeting this Pastor and maybe he can explain what I'm trying to tell you. You can hear it come straight from his mouth. It seems if I try to say anything your guard immediately goes up. Do you want to come?"

"No, Mahogany, I don't." Dawn flipped her long auburn locks over her shoulders. "I have been out of work too much." Even if she could go, Dawn wouldn't. "I'm sure you'll fill me in on whatever I miss."

"You're right, I will," Mahogany promised.

She could hear the sarcasm dripping in Dawn's voice. As long as Dawn dished it out, Mahogany could take it. A fire was lit within her soul to find out the truth. She would have answers to all her questions tomorrow. She could hardly wait.

*   *   *

Damien noticed Nicole from the moment he entered Cinelli's restaurant. She wore a tight yellow dress with a slit up the side. Her caramel colored skin-tone added a different dimension to the dress, a very tantalizing one. She waved him to a secluded table where she sat.

"And you thought I would be the late one," teased Nicole.

"I'm a whole five minutes late. Will you ever forgive me?" Damien placed a gentle kiss upon her hand.

"I'm only joking. I took the liberty of ordering us a chardonnay," smiled Nicole.

"Take whatever liberties you wish." Damien glanced over her features. The make-up she wore gave her an alluring look. Her braids were swept up in a delicate French braid. Gone was the "Mary Ann" look; "Ginger" was front and center. The waiter refilled her empty wine glass.

"Let's make a toast."

"What are we toasting too?" Damien asked.

"To new beginnings," their crystal glasses clinked. The mood of the restaurant had a relaxing atmosphere. Movie posters from the fifties covered the wooden walls and a Frank Sinatra impersonator sang "New York, New York" as he moved from table to table.

"What are you thinking about?"

"I'm thinking about what makes a woman like you tick?" answered Damien.

"The love of what I do. I love technology. It is a constant evolver. Technology never stays the same, I truly enjoy that."

"I figured as much. This latest contract with Digital Connections would undoubtedly change things in the world market, do you agree?" Damien questioned.

"I do. You probably know just as much as I do regarding the impact of the R.F.I.D. I read over the report you submitted to Michael. I have to admit, I'm a little jealous of your skills. The report was very impressive, Damien."

The waiter quietly returned with their food, Damien ordered the homemade vegetarian lasagna while Nicole had the typical spaghetti. Cinelli's was renowned for their authentic Italian dishes.

"Smells, good," commented Damien. "Can you think of any other reasons the R.F.I.D. could be used other than what I suggested within my report?" Damien watched Nicole's reaction closely as she briefly looked away.

"No. Why are you wondering what I think? The contract has already been signed. Phoenix Technology will buy Digital Connections per your proposal. I'm sure within the next couple of months. A millions of suggestions will come to the light."

Damien noticed that her skin was flushed from the alcohol. He refilled her wine glass in hopes of loosening her tongue to get her to talk about the conversation that he overhead outside her office.

"I tell you a secret," whispered Nicole. "The dermal R.F.I.D. will have uses beyond your wildest imagination."

It was the only time during the dinner she voluntarily made any reference to the R.F.I.D. Damien tried unsuccessfully to elicit more information from her, but she knew she made a slip and tried very hard to cover her tracks. Damien watched as she took another sip of wine and he called the waiter over for the check. At least the dinner wasn't a complete waste of time. Nicole did corroborate his belief that there was something amiss.

"Are you okay to drive home? Do you need me to give you a ride?"

"That would be wise," she agreed. It was hard for her to concentrate on the words he spoke.

During the ride home, the discussion became light. Damien found out that Nicole was a huge fan of basketball and had quite a devotion to Kobe Bryant.

"I couldn't believe he cheated on his wife," Nicole declared. "Think about it. He always portrayed this clean, nice guy image and then we find out he's not the person he appeared to be. That goes to show you, no one is as they seem."

"Well, we are here," Damien announced as he pulled up into Nicole's apartment complex. The drive was quicker than he expected. "Are you able to get in okay?"

"Yes, thank you for driving me home," Nicole grabbed her keys and accidentally dropped them on the floor of the car.

"Here, hand them to me," insisted Damien. "I'll make sure you get inside."

Nicole gave her keys to him as he escorted her up the steps. He found the correct key and guided her inside her apartment. Damien observed a large manila file labeled Stage Three Implementation of R.F.I.D. on her coffee table. He needed to see what was in that file.

"Why don't I wait and make sure you get tucked in," pressed Damien as he steered her towards what he assumed to be the bedroom. "Why don't you tuck me in?" Nicole murmured seductively.

She pulled his head down for a kiss. He could still taste the potent wine on her lips. Damien couldn't stop the age-old response from his body. Months had passed since he had been with a woman. The last woman he made love to was Mahogany. He remembered it vividly. The only thing he regretted was that their lovemaking was over too quickly. He wanted their passion to last forever. Strangely, he hadn't felt the urge to be with anyone else. However, months and months passed by without feeling a woman's touch. Now his body signaled more than gratifying sensations throughout his body that he could no longer ignore.

Damien returned Nicole's kisses more passionately, trying to consume her. They feverishly tore at each other's clothes until nothing stood between their bodies. Damien followed Nicole down onto the floor. His hands fumbled through his wallet for a condom, and he placed it on. Putting Nicole's hands over her head, he quickly covered her. The intensity of Damien's lust astonished Nicole. She cried out with each forceful move he made. Damien's breath hissed through his teeth as he lifted her body up against his. He let out a loud groan. He disengaged their bodies and noticed that although the sex was intense, it left him greatly unfulfilled. Rolling over, he found himself with one thing on his mind: Mahogany.

*　　　*　　　*

The parking lot of Calvary Fellowship was empty. Pastor Ethan agreed to meet Mahogany early that afternoon. The church building could easily house six hundred people. The glass doors from the main lobby area led directly to Pastor Ethan's office. A young gentleman led Mahogany to the Pastor's office. Pastor Ethan immediately rose to his feet. By reading his persona, Mahogany gathered that he had seen a lot in his day, his eyes seemed to hold plenty of stories. He used pomade to slick back his gray-black hair and his full moustache was trimmed to perfection. His tan slacks complimented his white Dockers shirt.

"Ms. Fox, it's nice to meet you."

"It's nice to meet you too, Pastor, but please call me Mahogany. I want to thank you for taking the time to see me. Joshua told me that you were leaving on a business trip pretty soon."

"It's not a problem. I had to come by here to pick up a few things for my trip to Washington D.C. Joshua told me that you had some questions concerning the Bible. Tell me how I may be able to help you."

"Well, to make a long story short, I was prompted by a disagreement with a friend of mine to find out why I believe what I believe. How do I know Jesus is real or even the Bible is true?"

Pastor Ethan grinned and was silent for a moment. When he spoke, his deep voice resonated throughout the room.

"First, let me say that faith comes by hearing and hearing by the word of God. You can read scriptures in the Bible 24/7, but unless you have faith it will be near impossible to believe. Your friend will have to come to believe the Bible on her own. With that said, what do you want to know?"

"Joshua had explained that you believed we were living in the Last Days," he held up his hand before he interjected, "the Bible teaches us that we know not the time or day of the end. Tomorrow is not promised to us. The true focus of the Last Days should be when we take our last breath."

Mahogany whipped out her pen and notepad to write down each bit of information Pastor Ethan offered.

"We are currently living in the church age," he rubbed the bottom of his chin. "First you must understand, mankind has been living in the heart of Last Days for the last fifty-five years. The U.N. declaring a state of Israel in 1948 was not a historical accident. It was the hand of God controlling the affairs of men just as His prophets said He would. The church age began at the birth of Jesus and will stop upon His return for His church, otherwise known as the rapture."

"Joshua said the same thing about the formation of the state of Israel," recalled Mahogany.

"The disciples asked Jesus what would be signs of His return and the end of the age. He told them there would be rumors of wars, nations rising against nations, and famines, pestilences, and earthquakes in various places. He told them that these signs would be the signs of the beginning of the end."

"And you feel that is happening in our lifetime?" Mahogany asked. She couldn't remember a day when there wasn't talk of wars or earthquakes and struggled to see the correlation Pastor Ethan tried to make.

"No question about it. Look at the news, there is corruption everywhere you look. I believe that God uses various ways to communicate with the spiritually deaf. America, as a society, has ignored His warnings. God has always warned the world of his coming judgments. He warned Noah of the coming flood, Abraham and Lot of the coming destruction of Sodom and Gomorrah, and Moses of the ten plagues on Egypt. Do I believe America was given a warning on 9/11? I don't know. Jesus announced His return would be during a time labeled 'as were the days of Noah.' During Noah's days wickedness on the earth was great and every intent and thought of man's heart was evil. Mahogany, newspapers and televisions are swamped with grotesque stories that would make your stomach turn. Parents murdering their own children, priest raping children, the Supreme Court protecting pornography rights, business fraud gone rampant, and same-sex marriages are now considered to be the norm. Have you found yourself asking what in the world is going on? Well, the Lord foretold us these things before they would happen. Prophecy validates every single word of the Bible."

"But how does Israel connect in all of this?"

"Once again look at the news. The Israeli/Palestinian conflict over land territory has spanned for centuries. Israel says that God gave the land to their patriarch, Abraham. The Palestinians say Abraham is also their father so the land is theirs. So goes the story."

"When do you believe the conflict will ever end?" questioned Mahogany. "Do you think America will be successful with the Road Map for peace offered by our president?" The Road Map for Peace treaty was covered by every news organization. "Finally Peace on the Horizon!" quoted the Washington Post.

"Amid the current war with al-Qaida and the Middle East conflict, never has the world searched for peace as they are today. Let me tell you, in 1st Thessalonians Apostle Paul cautioned there would be a global cry for peace during the Last Days."

Pastor Ethan opened the Bible that was lying on his desk and read aloud,

"'For when they shall say, Peace and Safety; then sudden destruction cometh upon them, as travail upon a woman with child; and they shall not escape.' Hallelujah! Can I get an Amen?"

"Amen," said Mahogany. "You were saying the conflict would end when?' she reminded.

"I didn't. Israel will only achieve peace when they accept Jesus as their Messiah. No 'ifs' and 'buts' about it. Understand that our president is putting our nation at risk forcing Israel to give away part of her land. The road map is doomed. The U.S. wants a Palestinian state to placate the oil rich Arabs and the Arab world wants a Palestinian state to eradicate the Jews."

"The President honestly seems to want to bring peace to the Middle-East, especially after the terrorist attacks."

"President Williams is the first US president who has ever publicly stated that he favored a Palestinian State. He was scheduled to deliver his comprehensive Middle East plan to the United Nations on September 13, 2001. As you well know those plans were cancelled."

"I don't see how you can say that when we are trying to help these people solve a problem that is obviously tearing their country apart."

"Don't take my word for it, read inside." Pastor Ethan turned the pages until he found what he was looking for. "And it shall happen in that day that I will make Jerusalem a very heavy stone for all peoples; all who would heave it away will surely be cut in pieces, though all nations of the earth are gathered against it. Hallelujah! Can I get an Amen?"

"Amen," responded Mahogany.

"When the Lord told Abraham, I will bless those who bless you and curse those who curse you. The United States is living testimony of that promise. Since our founding, America has stood firmly with Israel. Which country has received more prosperity than the United States? But I tell you the truth. Our nation's persistent pursuit of a Palestinian state will remove us from this blessing to a cursing. Our glorious mantle of world leadership will cease to exist."

"But it's not just America wanting peace, its other countries too." "Yes, there's the European Union, Russia, and other Arabic countries. However, we are on a dangerous course. A course our country has never seen before. We are the country that has chosen to remove God out of our schools, legalized the murder of innocent babies in the name of "choice", the ACLU constantly attacks Christianity while promoting secularism. We are constantly told we must accept other cultural beliefs. But let me tell you this, we are told to be neither lukewarm nor cold for the Lord, but hot in our fervor for him!"

Pastor Ethan looked at his watch.

"It's almost time for me to go, but I want to stress to you the fact that we were told to watch. The signs that Jesus described are obvious to the spiritually minded, but they are obscure to those who are worldly minded." He flipped the bible pages over, "Don't be left behind, for the rapture of the church is on the horizon. It may happen today, tomorrow, or even years from now. Pay attention to these words from the book of Mark, 'But of that day and hour no one knows, neither the angels in heaven, nor the Son, but only the Father. Take heed, watch and pray; for you do not know when the time is.' He closes with, 'and what I say to you, I say to all: Watch!'"

"Amen!" shouted Mahogany. Pastor Ethan nodded his head in approval.

"All I'm saying is in today's day and age, I keep hearing the discussion of how tolerance among faiths will contribute to a healthy coexistence for the world. There is a movement between Muslims and so-called Christians to maintain and strengthen a bond within the two cultures. People are becoming confused that the Muslim god, Allah, is the same as the God of Abraham, Isaac, and Jacob. This is apostasy. The God of the Bible does have different names, such as Adonai, El Shaddai, Yahweh, Jehovah, Elohim, but not a single one of His names is Allah. Our God teaches love and redemption. He sent His Son into the world to die for our sins. Contrarily, Allah tells people to sacrifice their lives in order to gain salvation. Mankind is being drawn into every kind of spiritual deception these days. This is a huge signal to the church body," declared Pastor Ethan.

"A signal to show…" began Mahogany.

"One, to be ready and two, to show that the Antichrist is on the scene. He will be a key factor in the installation of a one-world religion" he finished. "I don't know how long it will be before it is implemented. Bible prophecy is a hundred percent accurate but it never gives us an exact time. I know that you've heard of the mark of the beast. Everyone thinks it's a joke but it truly isn't. The technology has arrived for people to purchase items by the scanning of a tiny little chip called R.F.I.D. that stands for Radio Frequency Identification Data chip. We couldn't do that ten years ago. There are various things that have been spoken about and haven't yet occurred."

"Such as?" asked Mahogany. He glanced at his watch again.

"I hate to do this to you, but I must go. My flight leaves in a couple of hours," he got up from his desk and put a couple of items in his briefcase. "Syria comes to mind. Isaiah prophesied that the city of Damascus would be taken away from being a city and lay as a ruinous heap." He stared at her. "Damascus is still a city, so that is one prophecy that hasn't happened. Also, the solidification of the European Union, over twenty counties has since been added."

Mahogany wrote down the last point he made and packed her belongings away.

"Thank you, Pastor Ethan for meeting with me and have a safe trip." "Thank you, I will young lady. Take care and God bless you." Mahogany left with her mind racing around every little detail Pastor Ethan mentioned. She was both a little excited and a little scared of the information she learned. She would share her notes with Shanice, ever since Omar's attack she had been on a mission to spend more time with her family. Lucas spent the day with Shanice and her daughter since Mahogany was unable to contact Damien. He didn't call her last night, not that he did every night, but she had gotten used to his phone calls. She made a mental reminder to check on him to see what he had been up to.

*　　*　　*

The flight to Washington D.C. was a non-eventful one minus the turbulence. The pilot mentioned that the wind gust were between twenty and twenty-five miles an hour. Pastor Ethan's plane was supposed to land at 1:13 P.M. He traded seats with an old lady who claimed sitting next to the window made her queasy. Looking out his window, he could see a tiny building in the distance. It was the White House. Many people were mulling about on a beautiful Saturday afternoon. No doubt, Washington D.C. got rather busy with thousands of tourists visiting the State Capitol. He was thinking of paying the Lincoln Memorial a visit when a flash of light streaked across the blue sky. The light changed into a billow of smoke when it crashed into the ground near the State Capitol leaving an enormous crater. Pastor Ethan saw a plume of smoke stretched across the land. He helplessly watched as bodies dropped seconds after coming into contact with a poisonous gas. The strong winds assisted the toxic fumes by spreading the poison further into the city. Pastor Ethan lost count of the number of bodies strewn about. From his vantage point, he could see bodies on the ground blocks away from the origin of impact. He could not believe his eyes. He just witnessed a terrorist attack. The pilot came on the intercom.

"Ladies and gentlemen, we will not be landing at Dulles airport. Sadly, Washington D.C. has faced a severe bio-terror attack."

The stewardess's tried calming the pandemonium that soon erupted on the airplane. "Everyone, please understand, the airplane is high enough in sky, we will not be affected," said one flight attendant.

The pilot continued, "The FHA has given us a flight plan to land in Richmond, Virginia. We should be there within 30 minutes, please take a moment to remember those who were not as fortunate as us to escape death today."

The plane turned returned southward and sailed through the crisp afternoon sky. Pastor Ethan rubbed the back of the crying old lady who sat beside him and took one final look out his window. The haze of the gas snaked through the city blocks looking for its next victim. The image of a woman lying next to a stroller became imprinted in his mind. He shook his head in sadness, how many more warnings would his country ignore? Maybe America had surpassed the point of no return.

Chapter Three

"I'm surprised that you're actually here," remarked Trent. He watched Dawn take a seat at the diner they agreed to meet at. As he waited for her, he allowed his nerves to get the better of him. His hands were clammy.

"Why wouldn't I?" questioned Dawn. "You said that it was important, not to mention you flew all the way from Idaho to see me."

Dawn's voice was strong and firm, but more importantly it did not quiver. Her showing up was for one purpose: Prove to herself and Trent that no longer was she afraid of him. The last time they laid eyes on each other Dawn was on the receiving end of Trent's fist. He caused her to be fearful of her own shadow. Yet, one night after a beating, Dawn had a paradigm shift.

After listening to Trent's drunken tirades on how she would amount to nothing and how she was a miserable excuse for a woman for giving away her son, a ball formed in the pit of her stomach that grew into courage. She left Trent's abusive behavior behind and found the courage to begin a search for the child she put up for adoption. Dawn already believed that she was a terrible person, she didn't need Trent to drive a knife through her only weakness: their son.

"Dawn, it is important. But first let me say that you look stunning," mentioned Trent. He could tell that she seemed more confident with herself. Confidence suited her well.

"Thank you. Always the charmer," Dawn smirked. Trent's appearance hadn't altered much. She did not see an ounce of fat on his body. Always a stickler for the latest fashion trend, he wore cream colored khakis with a black vintage shirt.

"Seriously, I mean it. Let me get to the case at hand. I've asked you to meet me in person so that I could personally ask for your forgiveness. I know I've hurt you and I wish that I could take back the things I did to you, but I can't. I don't expect you to give me an answer immediately.

Matter of fact, the only thing I hoped is that you would show up and you did. You've already succeeded my expectations. I would understand if you were to say no to my request. Looking back, I can't believe the things I did to you. I apologize and I'm sorry."

Trent wanted to touch her hand but he knew Dawn would pull away.

"What are you doing?" she questioned angrily.

"I'm not doing anything," answered Trent. The butterflies in his stomach had finally ceased.

"Then what do you want? You must want something. You can't possibly think that you can waltz back into my life and pretend that everything is okay? Trent, you must have gotten really drunk to think of this scenario." She gestured towards the table they were seated at.

"Dawn, I haven't had a drop of liquor in a year and two months," he defended.

"Sure you haven't. I guess you are the new and improved Trent Royal. Gone is the abusive, verbal tyrant," she said through clenched teeth.

Trent was taken aback by her anger. But then again he shouldn't be surprised. He felt guilty for whatever the affects were due to the abuse she suffered at his hands.

"You have every right to be angry with me. I have no defense for what I did. If yelling at me will make you feel better or ease a burden you have, please do it. It's not wise to hold things in. Maybe that's why I'm here," he offered.

He removed the wind from Dawn's sails. She wasn't used to his placating attitude. She had a lot of unsettled anger with Trent. She didn't know if he was playing some kind of trick or a game and it unnerved her.

"I can forgive you if that's the only thing you want," started Dawn.

"It is. Trust me. It is."

Dawn looked into his eyes and did not recognize the man whom they belonged to. Trent seemed different, but somehow the same.

"Once I forgive you, what is it that you want next?" said Dawn.

"I don't know. During the past six months, I've been doing speeches for Alcoholics Anonymous. I should have approached you a lot sooner. You know me taking responsibility for my actions is one of the seven steps toward recovery, but I was scared to. That's funny, huh?"

"What is?"

"All those years I had you frightened of me and here I am terrified just sitting here and speaking to you." He let out a deep breath. "I guess it's the shame I feel every time I see your face. It's a tough pill to swallow."

"Why did you hurt me?" whispered Dawn. For years she yearned for an answer but never had the nerve to ask.

"To make myself feel better, lack of self-esteem, a sense of hatred I had for myself. I could go on, but what's the point?" He touched his finger to her hand. "I wish I could give you a specific reason for hurting you, but I don't have one. The sad point is I really don't know why I did it, Dawn. Sometimes people do things without thinking…"

"For over a year?" she retorted. "How did you know where to find me?"

"It wasn't hard. Mahogany's mother is a friend of some people I know. Her mom didn't know that I was looking for you so don't try to hold it against anyone. Everything happens for a reason. I wanted to find you and I did."

"You think about him too, don't you?" asked Dawn. They both knew she referred to their son. Dawn's direct statement threw Trent a little off guard.

"Every day," he declared and Dawn believed his words. "Maybe that had a big part of it." Dawn recalled the hitting began shortly after she put their baby up for adoption. "What kind of man, given the opportunity, wouldn't take care of his own flesh and blood? I'll tell you what kind—a cowardly one."

Through their sorrows, Dawn and Trent would forever have a bond. The only relief Dawn found in her pain was the fact she had someone to share the burden of the blame she placed on herself. She continued speaking, releasing a flood gate of feelings.

"Deep down, I blamed you for listening to me and your parents when I should have said something and not take the easy way out. That's what a real man would have done, right?"

She was at a loss for words. Dawn had no idea how Trent really felt about the adoption. After it was finalized, they never discussed the adoption again until now.

"You alone are not to blame for the biggest mistake we made years ago," offered Dawn. "I should have done something, too. We were both young and too dumb to fully understand the consequences of our actions."

"I never told you this before, but after he was born I saw you holding him in your arms. He was so small, tiny and I let him be given away."

"Trust me," Dawn said in a low voice. "I know exactly how you feel." "I find myself constantly wanting to know what he would look like today." Trent rubbed his eyes in frustration.

Dawn wanted to tell Trent about her efforts to locate their son. But, she did not know how much she could trust him. Instead she took a different risk by speaking from her heart.

"Trent, there are days which go by where I'm mad at myself, too. I tell myself that giving him away was the best thing we could have done. I still feel so terrible. I will regret my actions every single day of my life."

"I know, I know exactly how you feel, Dawn."

"Trent, I suffered through your abuse. Sometimes I wanted to give up, but I didn't. I forgive you for what you put me through, but I can never forget what you did to me. I can move on now and close this chapter of my life that we once shared."

He gently took her hands between his. The color contrast between their skin tones was striking, it always seemed a bit erotic to her. His dark and milky brown while hers was a pale vanilla cream.

"Thank you, Dawn for forgiving me. You'll never know how much this means to me. I am trying to turn my life around."

"Keep trying and never give up," she suggested. Trent appeared hesitant to question Dawn further.

"Let me ask you something. Your parents arranged the adoption? Do you think they have information that will allow me to contact the people who adopted him? I just want to see him."

"This is what this meeting was about? You wanted to see what I know about our son?"

"Of course, not, I meant every word I said to you." He was incensed and couldn't control the rising volume in his voice. "It's just that we began talking about it and I thought it wouldn't hurt to ask you. If you believe I have ulterior motives in asking you to meet me here, then don't tell me anything at all." Trent grabbed his coat and got up to leave. "Thank you for meeting me." Dawn watched him walk to the door before she stopped him.

"Trent, wait," Dawn asked. "Don't leave. I had to see what your motives were."

"And did you?" He placed his coat in a nearby chair.

"I don't know. Please sit down. I'm trying to follow my instincts. To answer your question, no. My parents do not have any information on our son. I've checked and double-checked. I haven't found out anything. I've been looking for him since I left you," confessed Dawn. "It's been a difficult search, but nothing has prospered."

Dawn and Trent spent two hours discussing their son. It was a warm conversation. Dawn detailed the ups and downs she experienced in her search. She didn't know how much she could trust Trent, but it felt so good telling him everything because he could relate to what she had been through. Only time would tell if it was beneficial to allow him to have access to her new life. She used their time together to see if he recalled anything special during the night of the adoption. Before leaving the diner, Trent agreed to contact Dawn if he remembered anything. To ensure that she wouldn't be followed, Dawn waited in the diner nearly twenty minutes after Trent left. She could never be too safe.

*   *   *

"Can't you type the story here at home just as well if you were at work?"

"No, I cannot, Shanice" explained Omar. "All my information and contacts are there. If I don't hurry up and leave, I may not have a job."

The bio-terror attack on Washington D.C. had caused the death of over seven thousand people and those numbers were early statistics. Every news organization in the world soon descended on the U.S. capital to cover the tragic event. News reports immediately speculated that it was Al-Qaida. Omar needed to get to his office quickly to hear what the word was on the ground. The United States had a lot of enemies, enemies who believed that they could take free pot-shots at America without penalty. Everyone would assume that Al-Qaida was the guilty party. Omar had a hunch that until he put all the pieces together everything wasn't as it appeared. Tomorrow was Monday, and it was one of the busiest news days. He needed to leave now if he wanted to get a leg up on his competition.

"You're right," conceded Shanice. "But I doubt you would be so inclined to let me leave for work after someone tried to kill me at my job." Omar pulled her in for a kiss.

"Listen to me, Ali is still in the hospital guarded by policemen. And, if he manages to survive, he will have a one-way ticket to jail. Mr. Exum offered me the option of staying home, but I know that I can accomplish more work if I'm at the office. I'll be okay."

"All right, keep your cell phone on," ordered Shanice. If I don't get an answer, I'm coming out to find you."

"You won't have to. I'll be home tonight," he promised.

"Don't forget, I agreed to meet Mahogany at Calvary Fellowship, so meet me there."

"If I have time, I will, baby. I love you."

Before he left, they took a moment to watch President Roy Dean Williams address the nation on the television screen. The dark circles underneath his eyes did not do much to help his appearance. He was emotionally drained.

"Today our country suffered a great loss of lives because of an evil bio-terror attack. My fellow Americans, I want you to know that we will find those responsible and bring them to justice. We are facing a new war in the 21st century—a classic battle of good against evil. We are fighting for the humanity of mankind. I'm aware many of you are frightened, please stay home and comfort your families. We are analyzing all the information and have in custody the parties responsible. Our armed forces are dedicated to the security of our nation. Rest assured that America will triumph over this dark and painful period as she has done so in the past. Thank you and May Divine Providence continue to bless our nation."

"Whatever happened to 'God bless America?'" asked Shanice.

"I know," agreed Omar. "The Supreme Court ruling came down last weekend that it is unlawful for any government establishment to make a public reference to God without the inclusion of other gods that people may worship. They cited the unfair alienation of other cultures as the reason. I would not have believed it if I hadn't heard it with my own two ears."

The telephone ringing jarred their attention away from the television.

"I better get going. I'll see you tonight, baby."

"Alright, be careful." Shanice locked the door behind Omar and answered the telephone.

"Hello, Mahogany." Looking at the telephone display panel, she read Mahogany's name. She loved technology.

"Hey, are you coming tonight?"

"Yes, I am, though I'm not sure if Omar is or not. The D.C. attack will take up a lot of his time at the office. Why such a short notice on the church meeting?"

"Sorry about that, but Joshua called and told me that Pastor Ethan, the Pastor of Calvary Fellowship was minutes away from landing in D.C. when the attack took place. He drove back to Raleigh from Richmond and decided to have an impromptu church service tonight."

"Do you know what it is about?" questioned Shanice.

"No, I don't," confessed Mahogany. "But I do know that Joshua told me that I did not want to miss what Pastor Ethan had to say."

"Is Damien going to be there?"

"I have no idea. I left a message inviting him, but I doubt if he shows up. He's been avoiding me like the plague."

"What about you and Joshua?" probed Shanice. "Any sparks going on there? You talk about him an awful lot."

"Well that's because he is a great friend. I tell you, you would be amazed at some of the information he knows about the Bible. Josh is a fascinating person," reflected Mahogany.

"Why did you invite Damien?"

"Hmm," Mahogany thought a moment before responding. "Basically because I want him to grow spiritually as I do, and, by inviting him to come, maybe he can take something from tonight and apply it to his life."

"Well, just be careful that you are doing it for the right reasons and not for your own reasons, okay? Damien has to want to grow on his own. You can hope, wish, and pray all you want to but until he wants to change, your efforts will be all for nothing."

Shanice's words echoed in her mind. Mahogany knew it was sound advice, but she always wanted a family. When she and Damien first began to see each other, everything in the world seemed so right. Yet when she found out about his womanizing behavior, she could not believe how blind she was to all the signs leading up to the truth. Mahogany could not see warning signs through the eyes of her lust for Damien. Mahogany tried ringing Damien's phone one more time before leaving for the church meeting.

Cars were parked along the side street. The voices of the choir permeated throughout the lobby as they sang. The white gloved ushers guided people to the pews. Mahogany took a seat near the back of the church. She propped Lucas on her lap and sat back, enjoying the music. She scanned the crowd for Joshua and spotted him near the front. Their eyes met and held each other's at the same time. He winked and gave a quick wave. Pastor Ethan made his way to the pulpit to begin his sermon. Mahogany saw Shanice and her daughter enter and take a seat not too far from her.

"As many of you know, I came close to losing my life in the recent terrorist attack in Washington D.C. I want each and every one of you to know that I am standing before you by no other reason than the grace of God. Obviously, my mission in serving the Lord is not yet completed. Those seven thousand people that were murdered yesterday should serve as an example to those sitting here that tomorrow is not guaranteed to anyone. How many of those people do you believe knew where their souls were going once they died? Ten, a hundred, a thousand, two thousand, maybe even four thousand? That would still mean there were three thousand lost souls, what a sad picture to imagine."

Pastor Ethan continued to reiterate his message of preparedness. It was simple and to the point.

"People get health insurance because they may need medical attention. People get car insurance just in case they may unintentionally hit another car. People even get life insurance because they may unexpectedly die and be unable to take care of their loved ones. But what about soul insurance? What happens to your soul when you die? Who is going to take care of you after your spirit has gone and left this earth? I have only one answer for you: Jesus. If you do not believe in Christ and are hoping against hope that your good deeds would be a factor in the hereafter, then I have something to tell you. Don't gamble with your soul. You've tried everything else this world has offered you. Christ has offered you everlasting life. Take his gift…it's free."

Mahogany could feel the uncertainty of the crowd throughout the church. Many were starting to cry. Maybe from fear of the unknown or from the frank emotion in which Pastor Ethan spoke. From the corner of her eye, Mahogany saw Shanice wipe her face with the back of her hand. As the choir softly began to sing, Pastor Ethan raised his voice to the melody of the music.

"I'm inviting you to come down the aisles and accept Christ into your heart. Romans 10:9 says that if you confess with your mouth that Jesus Christ is Lord and believe in your heart that God raised Him from the dead, you will be saved. Don't be content wandering around in the dark. Understand that Jesus died for you and He loves you more than you will ever know."

Shanice walked down the aisle holding the hand of her daughter. She was one person among many. Omar stood unnoticed in the doorway and walked down the aisle to join his family in giving his life to Christ. Mahogany could not help the twinge of envy she felt watching them. However, her emotions did not overshadow the events of the night. She was very happy for the both of them. They had been through a lot and, somehow or another they had ended up standing there as a family for the Lord. Miracles surely happen every day. A few of years ago, Shanice had a tumultuous love affair with a woman. Days earlier, Omar almost lost his life. Omar told Pastor Ethan he wished to become saved and praises erupted from the pews.

Pastor Ethan shouted, "Can I get an Amen for our new soldiers in Christ?"

The shouting and applause startled Lucas and he began to cry. He stopped when he spotted his father making his way towards them. Mahogany could not prevent the smile that erupted across her face.

"I'm happy that you made it." Mahogany wished that he wasn't able to tell how excited she was to see him.

"I'm happy that you invited me," he responded.

Damien picked Lucas up and held him close. Mahogany felt him briefly rub her hand before he gave his attention to the service. She consciously told herself not to get her hopes up by Damien's presence at the church.

From her peripheral vision, Mahogany noticed Joshua glancing at her. Yet, each time she tried to look at him, Joshua would look away. The night was developing into a very interesting one.

*   *   *

Damien carried Lucas into Mahogany's apartment. He had fallen asleep at the church and Damien insisted on carrying him inside. He claimed it would be a little difficult for her to carry Lucas since he was so big. Damien changed Lucas clothes and put him to bed. Expecting him to leave after he was done, Mahogany waited in the living room.

"That was simple enough," he commented in a low voice. "He didn't even wake up when I took off his clothes."

"He played hard today. He has so much energy for a little boy."

An awkward silence fell between them. Mainly because they both knew Damien's flimsy excuse to bring Lucas in was exactly what it was—an excuse to come inside.

"So what did you think of tonight?" asked Mahogany.

"It was nice," he stroked his goatee before commenting. "But I have something else on my mind."

"What is it?"

"You. I'm lost without you. I know I've told you this before, but I promise this time it's different. I've been feeling down the last couple of days and then I got your message about church service and decided to come. Let me tell you, nothing has ever felt so right. So, I'm asking you to give me and our family another chance."

The reasons Damien told her were partially true. He did feel lost without Mahogany. He simply did not tell her the reasons that led him to such a revelation. Ever since he slept with Nicole, he had lost sleep and couldn't eat. Usually he could love them and leave them. Nonetheless, his actions from that night lingered in his mind like a bad stench. He didn't even say good-bye to Nicole when he left. What really made him sick is that he didn't even know why he had sex with her. Was his destiny in life to go back and forth aimlessly between women? He was ready for something more and what made him feel so bad is that he already had everything most people only dreamt of—a family.

"Damien, haven't we been through this already?" Mahogany leaned back on the sofa. "I already know where the path leads. I don't want Lucas' feelings to get hurt when things don't work out as they usually do. I won't risk it."

"I'm not asking you to risk anything. I know you've taken chances on me in the past. So how can I convince you this time that I am for real?" He took a seat beside her and held her hand. Hearing the conviction in his voice, Mahogany still shook her head.

"Damien, it's not that easy. In answer to your question, there are numerous things I can think of that would have to happen in order for you to convince me to change my mind. First one being- your promiscuous behavior."

"Honey, something happened in my life that changed me and I choose not to lead that type of lifestyle anymore. There's nothing to gain from it," he responded.

"What led you to such a conclusion?" pressed Mahogany.

"I honestly can't say. The change happened in my heart. Please believe me. I wouldn't be sitting here in the middle of the night talking to you, wasting your time if I wasn't serious. Trust me. The terrorist attacks…I was thinking about our future, and then all those people died. I don't want to waste any more time."

Mahogany wanted nothing more than to believe him. But she had reservations, Mahogany was at a transition point in her life and if

Damien wasn't on the same page then what was the point of entertaining the thought of reconciliation. He could read her mind.

"Service was beautiful tonight. I can see us going to church every Sunday as a family and I can see us taking our marriage vows there. I want to grow old with you. I can't take no for an answer, Mahogany. I need you. Can I hold you tonight?" He read the hesitation in her eyes. "I promise that's all I'm going to do."

"That's fine."

The words flew out of her mouth before she could stop them. His request seemed harmless enough. She had a vulnerability towards Damien, but she was stronger now and would not allow the situation to get out of control. Besides, he gave her his word that he would not try anything.

Damien walked her to the bedroom. He stopped in the hallway to get a comforter from the linen closet. Once in the room, he removed only their shoes and covered their bodies with the blanket. He held her close from behind.

"Thank you," he whispered in her ear. An hour passed and both were sill awake.

"Mahogany," he pulled her closer to him.

His restraint surprised Mahogany. Any other time, he would have her clothes off by now. Her body was highly aroused. She waited in vain for Damien's touch, but it never came. Mahogany reasoned that if Damien only wanted to sleep with her, he would have tried to. Maybe he really did mean what he said. The only problem she had with him was that his words sounded too good to be true. She felt him against the lower part of back. Mahogany ignored the voice of reason screaming in her head and made a decision to throw caution to the wind.

"Damien," she called in soft voice. "Yes, what is it?"

"Okay." Mahogany turned around to face him. "Let's do it. If you meant what you said, then let's give it a try, but we have to take things slow. Just so we're clear, we are exclusively seeing each other."

"Yes, there's no doubt about it. You are mine."

"I want you to love me, Damien."

"I do. You know I do." He ran his fingers through her hair.

"I want you to love me with your body," she whispered and pulled him down for a deep kiss.

He took his time undressing her. He would never get tired of looking at her body—the same body which gave birth to his child. It was an indescribable feeling that made him love her even more. She placed her hands underneath his shirt and ran them down his muscle-toned back. He removed his shirt and tossed it into the corner.

"Mahogany?" he said huskily. Damien saw her hand fumbling in the nightstand for protection. "Honey, please."

He took her silence as a sign of acquiescent and saw her hand shut the drawer. Damien honored Mahogany's earlier request to love her with is body. Every touch, stroke, and breath conveyed the extent of his devotion to her. Tonight was meaningful for the both of them. Damien vowed not to ruin the new opportunity she gave him.

Not a word was spoken during the rest of the night. As they drifted off to sleep, both lovers contemplated the future of their relationship because the notion of the both of them creating a fulfilling relationship always seemed unattainable.

*   *   *

For forty-five minutes, Shanice watched Omar pace back and forth on the carpet, it was the only thing he had done since they returned from church.

"Omar, what is going on? Are you stressed about what happened at church?"

"No, not it at all," he answered.

Omar debated telling his wife what he knew. His contacts had come through with a wealth of information which turned his day into a wild and paranoid one. Information which made his stomach hurt just by thinking about it. Look at him now, he was a mess and could hardly contain his emotions. One minute he wanted to yell then the next minute he wanted to punch something from frustration.

"You wouldn't believe me if I told you," he replied.

"I would. What is it, Omar?" The tone of his voice terrified her.

"I found out who was responsible for the attack in D.C," he stated. "Who? Al-Qaida," guessed Shanice.

"No, it's a different terrorist group called Hezbollah, they are based out of Syria. You've probably heard of Hezbollah before. For the last three years they have been sending fighters to Israel to perform homicide bombings. They can now add bio-terror attack on United States of America to their résumé of atrocities."

"How do you know?"

"Because the U.S. government is planning a nuclear strike on Syria as we speak. The United States has known for years the extent of Syria's propensity for terrorism. The State Department even has Syria listed as a full state-sponsor of terrorism." Omar counted each offence on his fingers, "They provide a safe haven, headquarters, and financial support for terrorist activities. Not to mention, Syria hosts ten radical terrorist factions in its capital, Damascus, that's only in the capital."

"So why didn't America do something to stop them before this attack?"

"Oh, we did," he said sarcastically, "The Senate passed the Syria Accountability Act, which imposes tough sanctions on their country. Not surprisingly, Syria continued on a destructive path that could not be controlled. President Assad of Syria actively recruited guerilla forces to cross the Syrian border into Iraq simply to attack U.S. soldiers. His efforts to sabotage the rebuilding of Iraq and the Middle East peace process were ignored by our government, until now."

"I don't get it. Why would Syria attack us if we have been letting them get away with murder? Omar, it doesn't make any sense."

"Shanice, nothing makes sense. Who cares why they did it, they did it. Does it really matter why? The point of the matter is that seven thousand people are dead and the world, as we know it, will never be the same again and I'm absolutely terrified."

"Tell me why." She knew that he was not telling her everything. "Hezbollah wasn't working alone. Another county helped the sleeper cells get inside our country to release the deadly virus. It was our so-called friend, Russia. The United States has hundreds of GPS satellites all over D.C. As soon as the bio- toxicants were shot from the missile, the FBI found the origin within a matter of minutes. The person who fired it off is now in U.S. custody singing like a bird. Do you now understand what is going on? After we bomb Syria, Russia is going to know that they are next on the list. They will not stand around and wait for us to strike first. Russia already has more than enough nuclear missiles pointed towards the United States."

"I see why you are concerned," responded Shanice, "but I don't understand why you are so stressed."

"Maybe the concept of me not being able to protect my family has something to do with it. This place we call a world is driving me insane. I try to go to work and end up almost dead. I want my family to be able to leave this house without worrying if someone is going to hurt you because of me, or if some crazy man is going to detonate a bomb and wipe out my family."

"I want that too, but I'm not going to let fear dictate my lifestyle. I'm actually trying to bring another life into our family."

"I know, and how long have we been trying to do that?"

"Almost a year."

"Have you ever wondered why you haven't conceived?"

"I don't know why I haven't, but I know that I will. I believe that it would happen in due time."

"Well, Shanice, I think we should take it as a sign. Why bring an innocent child into a world like this?"

Shanice had never seen him so dejected. His crestfallen expression cut her to the heart. The impending nuclear threat was real as the air they breathed. For a moment, she regretted that he shared the information with her.

"Are you going to print a story on this?"

"Are you kidding? So people can run around like it's the end of the world?" He gave a cynical laugh. "I don't think so. The only thing I can do is pray and that is something we probably all should do."

*   *   *

The following afternoon, Mahogany stopped by Shanice's to give her the latest update on her status with Damien.

"I knew that you two would get back together," claimed Shanice, "What took you guys so long?"

"I don't know. Everything seemed to fit together after he showed up at church. Then he stopped by my apartment and the rest is history."

"Girl, I hope so. I want the best for you. If you think he is ready to offer you what you need then more power to you."

"Thanks for your gracious approval."

"Have you told your mother yet?" asked Shanice.

"No, not yet. I'll tell her when she comes down here. She and my dad are coming for a visit.

"Well that should be comical. How's the Bible research coming along?"

"Better than I ever hoped it would. You would be amazed how many current world events connect back to the Bible."

"So you're a biblical scholar now? Tell me then," Shanice grabbed her Bible and read a random verse from the Bible, "What does this mean?" She enjoyed bantering with Mahogany. 'Or do you not know that your body is the temple of the Holy Spirit who is in you, whom you have from God, and you are not your own?' That's 1st Corinthians six verse nineteen."

"Not sure, let me see it." Shanice handed it to Mahogany.

"Girl, I'm only messing with you. You don't have to look it up right now. I don't even know what it means."

The verse piqued Mahogany's interest and she wanted to know what it signified. She was reading it for herself when Omar came home.

"Hey baby. Hi Mahogany. It's nice to see you." He threw his keys on the coffee table. "You haven't been over in a while. Hello…Earth to Mahogany." Mahogany jerked her head up.

"Oh hey, Omar, I didn't hear you come in."

"I see that. What do you have your nose buried in?"

"The Good Book, your wife gave me a mini quiz and I'm trying to find the answer to her question."

"She's always trying to shake people up." Omar sat down on the couch and messaged his temples, "I am so tired today. I left work early because I have this massive headache plus my body aches all over."

"You want me to get you something to drink?" asked Shanice.

"No, I'll get it," said Omar. He stood up briefly before he crashed down onto the floor.

"Oh goodness, Omar! Omar!" shouted Shanice. She gently shook him until he regained consciousness.

"What happened?" mumbled Omar.

"You passed out. You don't remember getting up?" He had been so stressed out during the last couple of days. It should not come as a surprise that his body could not handle the strain. Shanice could barely handle keeping the information Omar shared with her a secret from Mahogany. She could only imagine the anguish turmoil her husband was going through.

"I probably only fainted. I didn't eat anything for lunch. Let me get some rest."

"No way! We are taking you to the doctor to be on the safe side. Don't argue with me on this Omar. I'm not playing. You are going to the hospital."

"Fine."

Shanice grabbed her coat and purse in record time. "Mahogany, I'll call you and let you know how the hospital visit goes, okay."

"Don't worry about it. Take care of your family. Do you need me to watch Chloe tonight?"

"No, she'll be fine with us. Hopefully the doctor will prescribe him some much need rest and relaxation."

Shanice ushered a reluctant Omar out the door. Mahogany began her usual route back to the office. Once at the Phoenix Technology building, she did not get out of the car. There was a nagging feeling in the back of her head and it wasn't about Omar. The nagging in the back of her mind had everything to do with the scripture she read at Shanice's house. She reopened her Bible and read some of the scriptures above the one Shanice had picked out.

Mahogany studied aloud, "Do you not know that your bodies are members of Christ? Shall I then take the members of Christ and make them members of a harlot? Certainly not! Or do you not know that he who is joined to a harlot is one body with her? For "The two," He says, "shall become one flesh." But he who is joined to the Lord is one spirit with Him. Flee sexual immorality. Every sin that a man does is outside the body, but he who commits sexual immorality sins against his own body. Or do you not know that your body is the temple of the Holy Spirit who is in you, whom you have from God, and you are not your own? For you were bought at a price; therefore glorify God in your body and in your spirit which are God's"

She was bought for a price. Those words seared Mahogany's soul. All of sudden, she felt shame over the way she lived her life. "Bought for a price" reverberated throughout her mind. At that moment, she truly felt ashamed- especially of those passion fueled nights with Damien. Mahogany started crying, but she didn't know why. The crying helped lose whatever emotional baggage she had been carrying around. Looking in the rear-view mirror, she saw that her eyes were a mess. She stopped in the ladies restroom to freshen up before heading up to her office. She will try to do better

As she stepped into the stall to blow her nose, she heard two ladies come in.

"Did he say anything to you?"

"Not a word. Every time I call him, he gives me a sorry excuse about why he can't talk because he has a meeting, or some B.S."

"Nicole, I still can't believe you guys hooked up. I mean, how do you go out for dinner and end up making hot passionate love on the floor of your apartment?" Both women shared a giggle. "Don't you feel strange working around him?"

"No, not really. I mean, it's not like he can fire me or anything," she laughed out loud. "That's okay. He'll come around eventually, especially after having a taste of the Miller."

"I don't know. He does have the reputation of being a ladies man. Don't get your hopes too high."

"He'll come around like they all do," gloated Nicole. "Trust me, Damien Andrews hasn't seen the last of Nicole Hunt." Mahogany stayed stone silent until the women left the restroom. Her cell phone began to ring.

"Hello," Mahogany answered in a broken voice. "Mahogany, Omar has leukemia."

Chapter Four

"Have you heard a response yet?" asked Gabriel.

"Yes, I have and I'm sorry. They say they don't have it," replied

Rabbi Levine.

Gabriel called Rabbinate Joseph Levine days earlier bursting with excitement from the news of the water flowing from the Wailing Wall. The first words out of Gabriel's mouth were "We must get them back." Rabbi Levine knew Gabriel referred to the first and second temple artifacts stored within the Vatican. It was a widely known fact that the Vatican storerooms housed the huge golden menorah and other vessels that stood in the Temple of Jerusalem two thousand years ago. For years, the Vatican denied that it held any sacred vessels. However, it was impossible for them to deny the truth when it was etched in stone. The Arch of Titus Pillar in Rome depicted victorious Roman soldiers marching off with the seven-branched menorah after sacking the city of Jerusalem in 70 A.D.

"They are lying. Rabbi, can you call for an investigation?"

"I know, Gabriel. I don't think so."

"It isn't going to stop us from our mission," declared Gabriel. "We already know where the Ark of the Covenant is located." A select few knew it was hidden in a secret tunnel near the Temple Mount.

Over his own personal supervision, The Shtiah Rock Assembly had prepared the vessels, and linen priestly garments required for future Temple services. Colleges in Jerusalem trained over six hundred descendants from the tribe of Aaron on how to correctly fulfill their future duties of Temple worship and sacrifice.

"The world community already has a tough enough time accepting the state of Israel. What do you think would happen if they heard that we were seeking the original golden menorah for the Third Temple? There would be a world outrage."

"The world's outrage is not my concern. Serving my Lord is. We must move forward and build the temple. Don't wait on the Vatican."

"I agree with you, one hundred percent," concurred Rabbi Levine.

"I've done my part. Rabbi please let me know if you hear of anything," Gabriel's voice had the sound of determination.

"I will my dear friend. Remember, the Lord works on His own time not ours—no matter how badly we want it. He and only He says when," finished Rabbi Levine.

Rabbi Levine hung up the telephone with a heavy heart and a feeling of impending dread. He was ashamed to admit it to Gabriel, but he was deeply afraid. Israel, his beloved country, was at a critical stage in history. For years, his people were persecuted for the simple fact they were Jewish. He wanted peace and a world to live in that his children could grow up without carrying the same burden of fear. Things looked bleak. The United States recently suffered another terrorist attack and now Gabriel asked him to risk Israel's safety by opening a can of worms. He stroked his beard. There was another option he could exercise. Rabbi Levine sat down at his computer and sent an e-mail to an old friend.

*   *   *

The Italian police stood guard outside of David Ibraham's room at the Vatican. The recent attack on his life had left him a little shaken. The Jordanian police department found those responsible for the attempt on his life. David's personal bodyguard was part of the scheme. His Arab brothers were angry with him given that the name, David Ibraham meant betrayal to their ears. He was the first Arab cardinal of the Catholic Church and he proudly used his position to promote solidarity among people of diverse faiths. The world had become ridden with violence often waged in the name of religion.

For his efforts, the Vatican saw fit to honor him with the highest honor—the papacy. The circulating rumors were true. David Ibraham was about to become the next Pope of the Roman Catholic Church. He could not believe it, but everything was nearly in place for that eventuality. It had taken fifty years for the players to take their parts on stage, yet only David knew how the final act would end. The year 1957 laid the key foundation for implanting the conclusive plan. During that year, six countries in Europe signed the Treaty of Rome—an agreement to bring all the nations of Europe together for the first time since the days of the Roman Empire.

"Cardinal, they are ready for you."

The soon-to-be absconding Pope John Peter II stood in his regal garment on the balcony of the Vatican in front of a crowd that easily topped half a million.

"I want to introduce a man of integrity, a man who continues to make strides to heal the rift that divides us as human beings. We almost lost him due to an assignation attempt. His works demonstrates the dream we share to live in peace. My flocks, my parish, please join me in welcoming your new Pontificate David Ibraham!"

A thunderous applause erupted from the sea of people below. David calmly walked to the podium wearing a white robe with a golden crown.

"Thank you, Thank you for your acceptance," David said in a booming voice, "Your acceptance of me will not go unacknowledged. Another deafening round of applause rose from the multitudes as David continued.

"I want you to know the attempt on my life will not bring to a halt to the commitment I have for a peaceful coexistence in this world, no matter what religion you follow. Tolerance must exist among Christians, Jews, Muslims, Hindus, Buddhist, Confucians, Catholics, Agnostics, Atheists, and everyone, in order to cultivate greater understanding, respect, and cooperation between the boundaries that separate us. I am not embarrassed to admit that one of my best friends is a Rabbi. Together we have prayed at the Wailing Wall in remembrance of the Holocaust. Ten years ago such dialogue would have been unheard of. Now a reconciliation between Jews, Christians, and Muslims is on the horizon. Our blessed mother, Mary, the Queen of Heaven has blessed us to live in a time of such great hope!"

Applause cascaded towards the balcony. The massive crowd chanted, "David!" "David!" "David!" He slowly raised his hand towards the audience asking for silence.

"My people know that I humbly accept the Pontificate position. I will guide you into an era of peace and safety. We can have a world without terrorism, we can have a world with peace between Jews and Muslims, and we can have a world without war only if we become tolerant of other's beliefs. Unite with me on this mission. Thank you! Thank you very much. Shalom! Grace be to Allah!"

David turned away from the podium exhilarated. He shook hands with the other cardinal's before heading back to his guarded bedroom. Once inside he locked the door and drew the curtains, immersing the room into total darkness. Walking over to the dresser drawer he removed two black candles and a vial of blood. After removing his garments, he rolled the large afghan rug into a corner and began to trace a pentagram with the tip of his finger on the center of the floor. Before sitting in the middle of the symbol, he placed a drop of blood on the wicks and lit both candles. He chanted until he fell into a deep state of his mediation. A knock from the door jolted him out of his trance.

"Yes?"

"Your Excellency, you have a phone call. May I put it through?" "Yes, you may do so."

Rising from the floor, David answered the phone when it rang. "Hello."

"David, this is Joseph Levine. I am calling to offer you my congratulations. I cannot think of anyone who deserves this position more than you."

"Why thank you, Joseph that means a lot coming from you. Especially concerning our history. Who would imagine two kids of questionable backgrounds turning out to be successful? One's a rabbi and the other turned out to be the Pope. I'm positive there is a joke in there somewhere," smiled David.

David had known Joseph for fifteen years. They met at an Inter-Faith Religious Dialogue gathering. Both men saw too much blood shed in their lifetime and were eager to find a way to end the tumultuous relationships among the Jews and Arabs. Not surprisingly, through their profession, both achieved their dream.

"I'm sure there is," remarked Rabbi Levine. "Sorry to change subjects, but I have a favor to ask."

"Of course. Anything you need I will do for you," assured David. "This is not easy for me to do. I have thought long and hard about coming to you, chiefly because of your new position. Nevertheless, I will ask anyway." Rabbi Levine took a deep breath, "I'm sure that you have heard the news of the water coming from the Wailing Wall. Israeli citizens deem this as a sign of the coming Messiah and wish to take the necessary steps to rebuild our temple. I'll get to the point. We would like the original menorah that once stood in our temple thousands of years ago."

"I see," commented David.

"I've contacted people at the Vatican prior to your appointment and they, of course, said that it wasn't there. But…"

"But you think we do?" prompted David.

"Yes, numerous sources have claimed they have seen it with their own eyes."

"I tell you a secret, Joseph" David said softly, "your sources were correct. And I cannot think of a better demonstration of unity to show the world than by giving the temple menorah back to Israel. Joseph, what a fantastic idea! Consider it done."

"The Lord must have hand-picked you directly for an hour such as this. Thank you, David. Generations to come will undoubtedly remember the name David Ibraham. I know you are a man of your word."

"I have some upcoming trips planned. When I return, the first thing I will do is make this wonderful announcement, okay?"

"Yes, yes, anything you need please let me know. I'm a little stunned right now because I can't believe it was this easy. Thank you, once again, David or shall I say you're Highness. I know you must be busy doing other important things. I'll speak with you later," remarked Joseph.

"You're welcome. I consider it an honor to assist you in any way that I can. We will speak again in the coming days, my friend. Goodbye." David Ibraham placed the phone back onto the receiver. He realized, he couldn't have planned it better himself. Things were moving so quickly. It was almost time for the grand finale, but the other pieces of the puzzle were not in place. He placed the candles and the vial back into the drawer and positioned his garments and headdress back on. He exited the room with the other cardinals following close behind. His true master was extremely pleased with his actions. It was show time!

*   *   *

The sun was setting over the Old City in Israel, it painted the blue sky a beautiful shade of pink. From the Mount of Olives, one could look down on the city as King David did during ancient times. It was the eve before the Sabbath. People bustled about trying to get the last of their groceries before the evening set in. Three years of the current Infitada war did not dampen the resolve of the residents of Israel.

No one noticed when the ground slightly trembled. The small quivers occurred several times a year and didn't give anyone cause for alarm. However, when the ground began to violently shake, widespread panic multiplied within the crowd. To no avail, countless people tried seeking shelter within nearby department stores. The earthquake was relentless in its quest for destruction. It leveled every building inside its path. The cities of Emek Refaim, Abu Tor, and Jerusalem were hit the hardest.

According to those who were able to witness it, the Al-Aqsa mosque split completely down the middle and collapsed into thousands of pieces. Nothing but a pile of rumble remained of the great building that once stood on the mount for over a thousand years. Seismologist measured the magnitude of the earthquake to be exactly 7.0. News of the earthquake's devastation spread like wild fire. Muslims around the world openly wept after hearing that their sacred mosque was reduced to a heap of dust.

However, one man fell to his knees in gratitude upon hearing the bulletin on the destruction of the Al-Aqsa mosque. Gabriel wiped tears from his eyes and said aloud in his native tongue, *"Ani yodea she elohim kayam biglal she hu shama at tfilotai livnot at beito!"*

When translated, the meaning of his words were, "I know that my Redeemer lives because He has heard my supplications to rebuild His house!"

Chapter Five

Dawn could not believe that she was sitting on another airplane. Trent called from Idaho with a promising lead regarding their son. Yesterday, Dawn's mother rang her during the night distressed because Trent paid them a visit. A visit which left her mother very uncomfortable to the point that they implored Dawn not to listen to a word Trent told her. She claimed he was full of lies. After speaking with Trent, Dawn learned that her parents withheld crucial information concerning the adoption. Trent wanted to tell her in person what he learned, plus they could follow up on whatever lead he got from her parents.

It took her three hours to get through airline security. The terrorist attack caused new and stricter security methods to be implemented. Airlines were not taking any unnecessary chances. Dawn didn't know how much information Trent had, yet she believed that it was worth the trip. Everyone knew that she would do anything to find her child, so it was rather difficult to believe that her parents did not share with her the complete truth. Did they hate their grandson so much they would lie to their own daughter? Her parents' reaction to her son was the driving force of Dawn's anger. How could they call themselves a family if they could treat an innocent child the way they did? Dawn wanted her own family—someone she could love unconditionally. That wasn't asking for too much.

It was hard not to envy Mahogany and Shanice. Both women recently rededicated their love to the men in their lives. Her last conversation with Mahogany left her feeling surprised. Dawn witnessed Damien's lack of judgment and lack of fidelity, yet Mahogany seemed to welcome him back into her life with open arms. Maybe Damien had changed, but Dawn believed that a leopard's spots never changed. The seatbelt light came on and the pilot informed the passengers that they would land in Boise in fifteen minutes. Trent was the first person Dawn saw upon exiting the terminal.

"Hello, Dawn, let me carry your bags for you," offered Trent. His hair was trimmed lower since the last they saw each other. He was nearly bald.

"Thank you."

Dawn tried reading Trent's facial expression to prepare herself for what he was about to tell her. They managed a little small talk in Trent's car until Dawn got settled in her hotel room and headed down to the lobby bar.

"So, tell me the big news."

"First tell me, do your parents know that you are in town?"

"No, Trent, I didn't tell them. Why does it matter?"

"Just curious, I guess you were following your instincts, huh?"

"I guess so."

Dawn sipped on her amaretto sour, allowing the burning sensation to briefly numb her senses.

"I'll get straight to the point. You're parents lied to you." Trent confided.

"About what?" Dawn asked.

"I was skeptical of the information your parents told you. So I decided to pay them a little visit. Well, I should say that I paid your mother a visit. I never told you this before, but she explicitly told me that our biracial child would have a horrible life growing up because of his race. She said I owed it to my son to offer him a better opportunity than I had. She produced papers on a well-to-do couple who couldn't have their own children and mentioned that it would be great if, from the mistake of your pregnancy, I could grant someone's wish to have a child"

Dawn didn't say a word as he continued.

"I started applying the pressure on you to go along with your mother's idea of the adoption. We knew that you could not stand up to both of us and forced you to sign away our child. I was very angry with myself, so I projected that anger onto you." Trent took a sip of his water. "Your mother lied to me when she told me that we would still be able to keep in contact with him via his new parents. A couple of weeks later, I went over to get the details on the couple and she acted like she didn't know what I was talking about or the names of the adopters. I called your mother a couple of times after that and she feigned ignorance when I told her I wanted to know where our son was. So I dropped it. Dawn, I had no idea you were searching for him. Once I got back here from Raleigh, I told your mother that she better tell you the whole story before I did. Of course, she said that you would never believe me and threatened to press harassment charges against me if I came by her house again. That's when I called you. I honestly believe that your mother is holding something back and, if you have a way of making her talk, I think now is the most opportune time. I can't describe it, but when I spoke with her, it was like she was afraid of something."

"Trent," started Dawn. "Part of me wants to be very angry with you and another part wants to be very grateful to you. Why didn't you tell me this before?"

"There never was a good moment. In high school, I believed it was best that I didn't say anything since you didn't show any interest in our son. We were both guilty of acting like we didn't have a child somewhere out there in the world. It was a learning experience."

"Yes, it was," Dawn agreed.

Dawn finished the rest of her drink. Her nerves were stressed to the max and deep down Trent still intimidated her. No matter how hard she tried to put up a brave front, she convinced herself that he had ulterior motives for getting her to come to Idaho. Although it did not seem like his style, it wouldn't be difficult to test her theory. Her mother was another story. Their relationship began to be contentious from the moment Dawn dated Trent against her mother's wishes.

"Trent, couldn't this have been discussed over the telephone? What was the urgency in getting me to come all the way here?"

"You want the truth? I didn't think you would believe me. Once you see your mother's reaction with your own two eyes, you will know why you had to fly here. But more importantly, I wanted to be present when you confronted your mother. I want to be there when you find our son, if you don't mind."

Trent read the hesitation in her eyes and he took a gamble on telling Dawn about a situation that forever changed his life. It was an experience that he rarely told anyone for fear of embarrassment.

"Dawn," he held her hand and refused to let go. "I am not the same man you knew two years ago. I must tell you what led me to stop drinking." Dawn sat her glass down, giving Trent her full attention.

"I'm listening," Dawn replied.

"One Friday night, I bought myself a bottle of tequila, brandy, gin, and vodka." Trent held his hand up showing four fingers. "I was hell bent on drinking myself into oblivion. I hated who I was. Was I trying to kill myself? I don't know," he confessed. "I drank all four bottles in a matter of hours. I just remember drinking and drinking until I passed out, probably from alcohol poison. But when I came to, I felt someone watching me. Have you ever had that feeling?"

Dawn nodded her head in agreement.

"I saw with my own two eyes these demons surrounding me. They slowly moved closer and closer to me when I suddenly saw these tall men wearing white robes standing with swords in their hands. The men holding the swords in their hands forced the demons back, like they were protecting me. The men with the swords never uttered a word. I would lose consciousness throughout the night and each time I awoke, the men continually had their swords drawn, daring the demons to make a move. Dawn, when I became fully awake, two days had passed. Two complete days, forty-eight hours were gone. It was late Monday afternoon before I finally became fully coherent."

"What happened?" asked Dawn.

"I don't know. All I know is that I'm alive sitting before you. I guess I have friends in high places," Trent joked. "But seriously, that moment changed my life like that." He snapped his fingers. "I was staring death in the face and didn't even know it. I was given a second chance and told myself that from then on I would stop wasting my life and make a difference in someone else's. So me asking to be with you when we find our child is simply that: a request from a man who wishes to see his son."

"I'm sorry. I know I may come across as overly paranoid." Dawn nervously played with the fork on the table. "The men with the swords, what did they look like? You're positive they or you didn't say anything."

Trent closed his eyes, trying to describe the picture in his mind.

"No, not a word was spoken. You know their faces were so bright I couldn't see them. Why do you ask?"

Dawn thought of the story Mahogany shared with her about the lady at her church. Both stories were eerily similar. They brought into focus the fact that a spiritual world does exist. Trent vocally discussing his near-death experience sent chills up her spine because there wasn't any scientific knowledge to back up their stories. On the other hand, Mahogany and Trent fundamentally changed their perceptions on life. Dawn could no longer deny the reality of a spiritual world—a world that seemed to fight the classic battle of good versus evil.

"I was just wondering," answered Dawn. "Who do you think they were?"

"Truthfully, I believe my guardian angels were protecting me."

"So do I," Dawn agreed.

"Do you want to wait until tomorrow to see your mother?" It was six o'clock in the evening.

"No, I don't think so. I wouldn't be able to sleep tonight if I waited. Why put off tomorrow what you can do today, right?"

"Don't forget the element of surprise," chimed Trent.

Trent took care of the bill before they left. The drive to Dawn's mother's house took forty-five minutes. If Dawn knew her mother, she was setting the table for supper. Janet Price's nightly habits were set in stone for the past twenty years. Lord forbid if one fork touched another one on the table. Dawn would face a ten minute lecture on her lack of direction. Her heart filled with dread in anticipation of seeing her mother again. Their last conversation wasn't exactly on the best of terms. After Dawn left Trent, she called her mother from North Carolina only to be told that if she hadn't dated outside of her race, the abuse would have never occurred.

"Do you want me to go in with you?" He told her his valid reason for wanting to be there. Now it was her turn to let him know how she felt. "I don't think so. I believe I can get more information if I see her alone. Will you wait for me out here?"

"Yes, of course," offered Trent.

Dawn nervously exited the car and walked up the cobble steps of her parents' home. She noticed the willow tree that stood beneath her old bedroom window. During high school, that tree provided Dawn a lifeline to Trent. When Trent threw rocks at her window, Dawn would climb down the willow to meet him. They would hold each other for a couple of hours before she went back into her bedroom. Dawn smiled in remembrance of how naïve she used to be. Taking a deep breath, she rang the doorbell. A few seconds later, Dawn heard her mother's familiar footsteps coming down the hallway before the door opened.

"Dawn? Hello darling, come in, come in. Why didn't you call and let me know you were coming? I would have prepared something special for you." Once inside, Mrs. Price gave Dawn an obligatory hug. "When did you arrive?"

"I got in a couple of hours ago. Where's dad?"

Dawn watched her mother as she finished setting the table. Her mother's appearance hadn't feathered well over the years. Her sullen skin was paler than usual and her hair was now totally gray.

"Oh, you know he's downstairs watching Jeopardy. He'll be up in a few minutes. To what do we owe your visit, my dear?"

"I spoke with Trent yesterday," began Dawn. Mrs. Price added a plate to the table for Dawn. "He said that you have information about the people who adopted my son."

"Why would you bother believing trash like that? I told you when I called that he was full of lies. Don't tell me you wasted a trip here because of him?"

"I did," confirmed Dawn. "Did you ever tell Trent about a couple who were unable to have children? Trent said you mentioned a quote unquote 'well-to-do' couple that wanted to adopt our son."

"Dawn, I'm telling you those accusations are untrue. Don't you think that if I had some information that I would have told you by now?"

"No I don't. Mother, that's why I'm here, hoping you would finally tell me the truth."

"I have told you the truth. You need to think about who has the most to gain by feeding you these lies. It isn't me. It's the man that abused you. He's trying to gain your confidence and get you back to where he had you before and I can't believe you fell for it. Go figure." Mrs. Price skin crawled every time she thought of Dawn being with that degenerate. Her deepest fear was that her church friends would find out about the skeleton in her closet. A bi-racial grandchild! She would never live it down.

"Yea, neither can I. I guess you're right."

Dawn felt stupid for even bothering to speak to her mother. Turning away, she started for the door. As her hand touched the doorknob Dawn spun around and confronted her mother.

"How dare you! How can you act as if you don't have a grandson in this world? How can you sleep at night knowing a part of me, a part of you, is out there in the world? Don't you want to see what he looks like? Is the love in your heart so cold that nothing can melt it?"

The sound of her mother slapping Dawn across the face echoed throughout the kitchen.

"I am your mother and I demand your respect! Do not enter this house questioning me on something that happened years ago. Something which has put a dark shadow over this family because of what you did because you couldn't keep your legs closed. Dawn, I love you. I am telling you as you mother, I do not have any information on the location of your son." Dawn allowed tears to fall freely from her face and spoke in a hoarse voice.

"It terrifies you that I want to find him doesn't it? After all these years, you still care what people think of you. You don't love me. The only person that you love is yourself. Your actions speak far more loudly than your words. Tell dad I'm sorry that I couldn't stay longer. Goodbye."

"Don't be sorry, Dawn. I'm right here," Nicholas Price enveloped his daughter within his arms, "and I heard the conversation between you and your mother with a heavy heart."

"Don't worry about it, Dad. I love you," said Dawn. She wiped her eyes with the back of her hand. "I wish I could spend more time with you, but I've got to run."

"I love you too. I apologize for failing you as a father. I should have given these to you a long time ago and I hope you can forgive me." He placed a stack of letters into her hand.

"Nicholas, No!" Mrs. Price ordered. "How did you find them? You went through my personal belongings!" Mrs. Price accused.

"Janet, be quiet. It doesn't matter, just know that I did. You should be ashamed of yourself. Have you no compassion? I'm getting up in age and have come to realize that, I have done some things that I'm not proud of. If I had the ability to go back in time to change them, I would. Janet, my baby girl is hurting and I will do anything within my power to ease her pain."

Mr. Price added, "These letters arrived within a couple of months after the birth of my grandson. There seems to be some recent ones in there too. I hope they will be of use to you and pray you will forgive me."

"Thank you, Dad. For the record, I do forgive you."

Dawn placed a kiss upon her father's cheek and brushed past her mother to the door.

"Dawn! Don't do this to yourself. You are going to open a can of worms that you can't handle!" shouted Mrs. Price. The sound of the door slamming was the only response she received.

Trent saw Dawn walking briskly towards the car and started the engine. From his vantage point, he could see that her eyes were red. She opened the passenger door and ordered him to drive.

"I guess things didn't go so well," probed Trent.

"Actually they did. I'm trying to process everything. My mother tried to tell me that you were lying to me and I almost believed her," Dawn said matter-of-factly. "There she was in the kitchen, Mrs. Cool, Calm, and Collected. She had her story together each time I tried to catch her in a lie. I believe that she hates that I'm her child."

"Even though I am very familiar with your mother," reasoned Trent, "that's a pretty harsh thing to say."

"She knew where he was, Trent."

"She admitted it? I'm so surprised." Dawn laughed aloud.

"No, she did not exactly admit it. My father gave these envelopes to me. They are from the people who have our son."

Trent pulled the car over to the side of the road. "Dawn, why haven't you opened them?"

"Because I'm scared. That's why," she answered.

"Let me see them and we can open them together," tried Trent.

He gently pried the letters from Dawn's hand and placed each envelope in order according to the postage dates. There were ten unopened letters in total and the return address on the letters had the name Fitzgerald as the sender. The first of the letters detailed how Trent and Dawn were more than welcomed to visit their child, little Nathaniel Fitzgerald.

"Nathaniel is his name," Trent said in a low voice. Trent could not remember the last time he cried, but he did so at that moment.

"My little boy's name is Nate." He repeatedly said over and over. Several of the envelopes contained pictures of Nathaniel. One seemed to be soon after his birth and the other two photos were of what seemed to be of his birthday party.

"He looks just like you," commented Dawn. "He has your eyes and dimples."

"I have to agree with you on your fine observation. I wonder why your mother kept these after all these years." Dawn picked up the last envelope.

"So do I. Trent, look, this one has a postal date just two weeks ago." Dawn tore it open and her hand holding the letter began to shake. "Oh my goodness, Trent."

"What does it say?"

"It says: Dear Mrs. Price, I hope that you will respond to this letter since you have never answered any of my previous ones. I have been diagnosed with breast cancer and my husband was my rock and strength. Unfortunately, he recently passed away in an automobile accident. Neither of us has an extended member of family to care for Nathaniel. I'm in the late stages of chemotherapy and have grown too weak to fully care for him. He requires and deserves more attention that I can give him. He will be placed in the state's custody since I am unable to care for him. I welcome you to come and get to know your wonderful child. Perhaps even to grow to love him as I did. Please give me call at 208-555-5791. Sincerely, Nina Fitzgerald."

"The return address is listed in Boise. Trent, my tip had a lead that led to Boise, I even had Nina's name and I could not find any trace of her. We have to find her."

"Don't worry, we came this far and I believe we made it thus far for a reason. We will call the number and see where that leads. Don't give up the faith now."

"I won't," promised Dawn.

Trent started the engine and merged into traffic. He would find his son. Maybe the search for his son would be the catalyst that reunited him and

Dawn. Trent knew he faced an uphill battle, yet it was one of his deepest dreams to have a family. During the past year, he never felt so alone in his life. He had nothing to live for, but that all changed once he confronted his demons with Dawn. Since speaking with her in that café in Raleigh, an open dialogue emerged between the two of them, a dialogue which could solve the mystery of their son's location. Even though he and Dawn had no idea on where the next road would take them, they welcomed the possibility that neither of their lives would ever be the same again.

*   *   *

"I thought I would hand deliver these signed contracts," Nicole offered seductively. She stood in Damien's office doorway. "What? Did you believe that you could avoid me forever?" questioned Nicole.

"I'm not avoiding you," Damien lied.

The truth of the matter was he never wanted to see Nicole Hunt again. Her presence constantly reminded him of the terrible decision he made. Damien could not put all the blame solely on her. He knew better than to mix business with pleasure.

"I have been swamped with these contracts."

"And the messages I left for you? I guess you are going to say that you never received them, huh?

"No, I'm not. I did get your messages, but…"

"But what, Damien? Don't tell me that you are the type of man to run and hide just because we had sex. Are you that uptight?" Nicole joked. She was a little hurt that he did not call her back.

"No, that's not it, Nicole. Not at all." Damien looked into her eyes. It was the first time he had done so since their night of passion. "Do you want the truth?"

"Nothing less," answered Nicole.

"In all honesty, I did not want to give you the wrong impression. I apologize for not returning your phone calls, but I did not know how to tell you that I only wanted us to remain friends, nothing more."

After speaking the words aloud, relief soon flooded Damien's body. He would try to correct the wrong he committed. Mahogany stood foremost in his heart and he knew that there was no time like the present to show it.

"Friends instead of lovers you mean?"

"Yes," answered Damien. "I think that would be best, especially since we work together." He knew his request would not be a popular one.

"Really? I guess you failed to follow your own advice when you banged me on the floor of my apartment," shot back Nicole.

"Nicole, please. Let's try to remain professional about this." He put some files away. "It's not like I had to twist your arm to do what we did."

Damien suppressed his frustration. He was so angry with himself. If only he had never entered her apartment. Everything changed once he saw that R.F.I.D file on her coffee table. He had hoped she would eventually pass out so he could go through the file. But, he let things get out of hand by allowing his body to control him. After he placed his clothes back on, Damien did manage to look inside the folder. The details of which bought up more unanswered questions.

"You're right, Damien. I also need to apologize for my behavior. Rejection isn't always the easiest pill to swallow, but, I will. I would like for us to remain friends. I have a suggestion. Why don't we pretend that night never happened?" she extended her hand to him. "Deal?" Damien saw that she was desperately trying to save face.

"Deal," he agreed. "I do need to say this: I apologize for acting like a cad. You are a very beautiful and intelligent woman. You already know this, but I'm going to say it anyway. Nicole, any man would be lucky to have you as his woman."

"Except Damien Andrews?" Nicole mentioned with a forced laugh. "Okay, I'll stop harassing you. Let's talk about something else. How are things going here at the office?"

Damien used the opportunity to subtly bring up the topics he read within the manila folder at Nicole's house.

"It's going pretty well actually. I have learned more about these

R.F.I.D. chips." "Like what?"

"Please have a seat, so I can go over it with you." He smiled at her, "Your smart little mind probably already knows everything I'm about to tell you."

"Try me," she teased.

"Well for starters, I had no idea that twelve years ago, the Ford Motor Company introduced an R.F.I.D. prototype immobilizer to pre- vent automobiles from being stolen."

According to Nicole's R.F.I.D. file, the implementation of RFID in automobiles and pets was Stage One R.F.I.D.'s.

"Damien, you get an A plus on your research. Ford's prototype was only known to a select group of people. And yes, I was already aware of it. It tested very well in their private sector market and a few years later Ford chose to expand on it. What else do you have?"

"When I had my meeting with Michael and Bart, I have to admit that I failed to think outside of the box. Do you know what other systems are using R.F.I.D's?" Damien hoped she would take the bait.

"Is this a test to see if you know more than I do?" Damien gave her a hardy laugh.

"Maybe? Consider it a pop quiz"

Nicole still had a difficult time not being drawn into his gorgeous eyes. She was jealous of the woman who captured his heart. Although he did not come straight out and tell her, Nicole could tell when a man was in love. Too bad it wasn't her.

"In that case, let me put on my thinking cap. The government has an extensive R.F.I.D. system that is used for toll collections." She absentmindedly played with a tendril of hair that escaped from the bun. "Another system is the Exxon/Mobil's Speed Pass. By waving a sensor attached to the key chain, drivers are allowed to have a fast and easy transaction after pumping gas. Libraries use them to keep track of books. Also, building securities use them to keep track of employees' location. The chip is imbedded within the name badges the employee wears. Did I pass, Professor Andrews?"

"With flying colors, Ms. Hunt."

Nicole knew to the letter, what Stage Two of the R.F.I.D. implementation included. The only thing that puzzled Damien was who had the time and money to strategically put together a system that gradually compromised individual's privacy.

What disturbed Damien the most were the transcript pages located in Nicole's file. He read pages and pages of transcribed conversations. It appeared that Digital Connections managed to perfect the greatest eavesdropping tool ever created. Not only did the R.F.I.D. assist in tracking consumer usage data, its receiver emitted a signal that allowed the readers to listen in on customers private lives.

Stage Three was listed as the final plan. The plan called for a gradual implementation of R.F.I.D.'s in all global products and for all countries of the world to implore their citizens to be tagged via R.F.I.D.'s.

"Do you think there will be a time when everyone would want to have an R.F.I.D. implant?" Nicole gave a nervous laugh and suspiciously eyed him.

"I really can't say. One never knows what the future holds. Why do you ask?" she inquired.

"I was just thinking. The potential for R.F.I.D.'s seems endless," Damien answered.

"That is very true. Now, do you wish to tell me the truth as to why you were pumping me for information?"

"There isn't any hidden agenda. I simply wanted to speak with you about a subject we are both very familiar with. Besides we are going to be working closely until every deal is signed," he quickly covered. "Now, you are starting to make me think you have something to hide."

Nicole decided to let the matter drop. Yet she still felt that Damien's line of questioning was a bit perplexing.

"Sorry to disappoint you, but I'm as open as they come. You, of all people, should know that," she smiled. Unsure as to how to respond, Damien turned his head away. "Relax Damien, I'm only teasing you for turning a good thing down."

"I know I deserve it," he replied.

"I would love to stay here and make you feel guilty, but I must go now." Nicole rose from her chair.

"Thank you for stopping by Nicole. I greatly appreciate your sense of maturity and do value your friendship. Can I at least have a hug? I truly regret how I handled things between us."

He held his arms open as Nicole walked around his desk and into his arms. She knew it was a regrettable action when she did it. Her body responded to his the same as it did the night they slept together.

Nevertheless, she quickly left the warm embrace of his arms. "I'll be seeing you around, Damien. Take care."

"I will. You do the same," he answered back.

Nicole left Damien's office and immediately reached for her cell phone. Alone in the elevator she placed an international call to Rome.

"Pontificate David, please? This is Nicole Hunt." Minutes passed by until the operator connected the line. "David, I believe we may have a problem on our hands." She wanted to know how Damien learned that the ultimate plan was for every person in the entire world to be injected with an R.F.I.D chip.

*   *   *

"Would you like something to drink?" "No, thank you," answered Shanice.

"Your husband should be back any minute. Dr. Rafti wanted to run a few more test before the end of the night. Mrs. Miller, you should know that the doctors caught the leukemia early. In my line of work, early is a very good sign."

"I hope so."

The nurse left Shanice to be alone. It was the first private moment she had to herself. Mahogany had stopped by earlier after Shanice called and told her the devastating news. Thankfully, she provided a shoulder Shanice could cry on. Omar needed her support not her tears. It was hard to contain the range of emotions that consumed her. How ironic! Omar escaped the clutches of a deranged madman only to end up facing death once again from a deadly disease. He wouldn't be able to leave the hospital for at least week. Her cell phone rang drawing Shanice from her thoughts.

"Hello."

"Shanice, this is Yasmine."

Shanice immediately recognized the voice from her past. She wished that she could forget the history they shared. Flashbacks of the time and passion they shared flew across Shanice's mind. She began to feel nauseous.

"Yasmine, what are you doing calling me?" whispered Shanice. All the trust she earned from Omar would vanish into thin air if he knew she spoke to Yasmine. Knots instantly formed inside her stomach.

"I read in the newspaper about Omar being attacked. Is he okay?"

"As well as can be expected," Shanice replied. She didn't give any more details. The sooner she ended the call the better.

"I only called because I wanted to make sure you were doing fine," her voice dropped. "I miss you, Shanice. Can we meet up this week?"

"No. I don't think that is a good idea," countered Shanice. She could hear Omar's voice down the hallway.

"I won't take no for an answer. Please," Yasmine said in a soft voice. Shanice's heart skipped beat when a nurse brought Omar back into the room. She tried not to show any nervousness in her face or voice as she continued the conversation. The nurse helped settle Omar into his bed before leaving the room. Omar turned the television on to see if he could learn more about the impending war.

"Let me see what I can do and I'll get back to you," Shanice said before hanging up her cell phone. She took a seat next to Omar's bed and asked him how the tests went.

"Not too bad if you wished to be a pin cushion. I had needles and tubes sticking everywhere out of me, baby, I'll be so happy when all of this is over," murmured Omar. "Hey, who was on the phone?"

Shanice felt the familiar knots rise within her stomach. The only difference from before is that the sensation was ten times worse. She promised herself that she would never lie to Omar again, no matter what the circumstances were. If she told him the truth, it would unnecessarily reopen old wounds. If she didn't, she could be ending her marriage. Choosing to honor her word, Shanice took a deep breath and began to answer his question.

"It was…"

"Oh my lord, Shanice, look at the television!" directed Omar. Shanice looked at the screen. The television showed live footage on what was left of the city of Jerusalem. The city was completely obliterated. The caption on the bottom of the screen read, "Devastating 7.0

Earthquake Rocks Jerusalem—Completely Levels Al-Aqsa Mosque, Death

Toll Unknown." A GNN reporter interrupted the broadcast.

"Ladies and gentleman, we have some late breaking news from President Roy Dean. We will cut to the White House now."

The television changed into a split-screen image of two items: one side showed the President of the United States and on the other: U.S. military fighter jets. Omar turned the volume up so they would not miss a word the President spoke.

"Citizens of America, I come to you tonight with a heavy heart. Due to the terrorist attack, our nation mourns the loss of over seven thousand citizens. Our National Intelligence Agency determined the group responsible for this atrocity was Hezbollah. I ordered our military fighter jets to destroy Hezbollah terrorists training camps. Their training bases were located in the Bekaa Valley of eastern Lebanon. As our US special forces entered the Bekaa Valley, they were met with heavy enemy fire. Furthermore, the President of Syria ordered his army to attack our soldiers. For years, the United States and the United Nations has tried to persuade Syria to abandon its affiliation to Hezbollah. Syria refused to do so. For years the world community has pressured Syria to discard its weapons of mass destruction and withdraw its terrorist groups from Lebanon. Syria refused to do so. For years, the United States demanded Syria to crush Hezbollah and put an end to the terrorist infrastructure within its country's capital, Damascus. Syria has refused to do so. Facing the threat of another attack on our homeland and the bold hatred Syria has shown our country, I have ordered a nuclear attack upon the city of Damascus. We are living in a very different world than our grandparents did and have no other choice but to fight evil by any means necessary. May Divine Providence continue to bless each and every one of you."

Omar put the television on mute as GNN simultaneously showed aerial footage of what was left of Jerusalem and fighter jets dropping what appeared to be nuclear bombs on Syria.

"Boy, if I didn't know better, I would say the end of the world is fast approaching. Remember what Pastor Ethan told Mahogany? He told her the Bible prophesied that the city of Damascus would lay as a ruinous heap," she remarked. Shanice held tight to his hand and said a little prayer. The Lord had given her a reprieve from answering Omar's question. If only He could ensure that Yasmine would never contact her again. Her impromptu phone call would have Shanice walking on egg shells for days to come.

Chapter Six

Mahogany curled up on the sofa with her pen and paper. The old saying, 'When it rains, it pours' replayed in her mind. What a day it had been! Shanice sat at the hospital worried of what the doctors would say about Omar's health while she settled down at home nursing a broken heart. The more she wrote, the better she felt. It was weird hearing Damien's escapades through the grapevine. Up until now she wasn't exactly sure how she would react to the news. Not surprisingly, she was angry with herself, angered at the fact that she gave him one more chance to prove her wrong. The early discovery of Damien's tryst was the only thing to be grateful for. At least she had not invested any more time than she already had. She invested her love, time, and energy into Damien. Her love for him was like a weed. No matter how bad she wanted to uproot and kill it, it would find a way to grow. She scribbled a few more sentences down before the doorbell rang. She knew it was Damien. He called her before leaving the office. Rising from the sofa, Mahogany opened the door.

"Hey Babe," he bent down to give her a peck on the cheek.

His eyes followed Mahogany. He couldn't help but notice that she seemed tired as she stared at him with her big brown eyes. He was so excited about spending time with her and his son. After his discussion with Nicole, he could not wait to get home to see his family. Family, the word alone carried a huge weight behind it. Nevertheless, he was more than ready to carry it. Driving to her place, he realized the sense of liberation he had after explaining to Nicole how he truly felt. His new devotion to Mahogany allowed honesty to flow through his veins a little easier.

"Hey," Mahogany said before she returned to the sofa. "Where's Lucas?" asked Damien.

"He's asleep. We've both had a trying day," she responded.

"Why? What happened?" He took a seat beside her.

"You wouldn't believe me if I told you."

"Try me," Damien asked.

"Well for starters, Shanice found out that Omar has leukemia and I had the lovely pleasure of finding out that you have been sleeping with some woman named Nicole. I would categorize that as a trying day wouldn't you?" She turned her body to face him.

Damien's blood ran cold and he put his head down in shame. He couldn't think of anything to say. He knew words at this point were futile to Mahogany's ears.

"How long have you been seeing each other?" Mahogany asked in a calm voice.

"We haven't. It happened one night and one night only. It's just something that happened. We are not emotionally involved with each other."

"Oh, I see. You are just sexually involved with each other correct?"

"Mahogany, what do you want from me? What do you need me to say? Tell me and I'll say it," demanded Damien.

"There's nothing you can say, Damien. Seriously, is there anything to be said that can fix this? I don't believe so."

"So what are you telling me? The words we said to each other a couple of nights ago don't mean anything to you?"

Mahogany's voice rose in anger.

"Damien, don't you dare try to flip the script on me. You are the one who can't seem to keep your pants zipped up. That's the reality of your life story," she remarked.

"It's your reality if that's all you continue to see in me, Mahogany. We were not together when I slept with Nicole and for you to sit here accusing me like we were, isn't right. I admit that I did not make a wise decision, but it's not important enough to throw away what we had."

"Were you going to tell me about her?"

"Probably not, there wasn't anything to tell. If I were going to tell you about her it would have been in the context of me confessing that I am nothing without you. The careless, empty sex I had with her led me to understand how unfulfilled my life has become. I had nothing to show for it."

"It took Nicole to teach that to you?"

Damien could hear the hurt in her voice. He could recall numerous times Mahogany implored him to change his womanizing behavior.

"Mahogany, you could want and hope for me to change all you want. But until I decide, until something inside of me transforms, absolutely nothing will happen. I apologize for hurting you once again. If it's any consolation, Mahogany, I did not intend to sleep with her."

"So what happened? What were your intentions?" She watched him run his fingers through his wavy hair.

"Well, Nicole is the personal assistant of the CEO, Michael Reed. I overheard a conversation she had on the telephone that piqued my interest. So I invited her out to dinner hoping to find out more. She got a little tipsy, I took her back home to make sure she got in safely and I was standing outside her door when I saw a file on R.F.I.D.'s."

"R.F.I.D.'s? The data chips?" Mahogany thought of her discussion with Pastor Ethan.

"Yea, you're familiar with it?" Mahogany nodded her head as he continued. "I went in hoping to sneak a peek at the file and one thing led to another. I apologize for damaging what little amount of faith you had in me. For that, I am deeply sorry. Don't give up on us because of this."

"Damien, I need to think about it. Really I do. Maybe you are not ready for a commitment and this was a sign that we need to heed," she absently scribbled on her notepad. "I don't know. It's a lot for me to analyze. You tell me one thing and then all of sudden I hear you're doing another. Not to mention, you work with her every day. I'm not sure I can do it, let alone want to do it."

"Mahogany, I have already told her that I wanted nothing more than to be friends. I was very direct and to the point. Nothing would ever happen between us again. I know I sound like a broken record, but I am for real. Don't hold something I did in the past against me because we will never be able to move to our future."

"I understand what you are saying, Damien. But what about the way I feel? I can't ignore that. I need some time alone. Can you leave? Please."

"Mahogany." He tried kissing her, but she jerked away. "If you want me to leave, I will."

"I do," she whispered.

Damien rose from the couch and planted a kiss on her forehead. He didn't say a word and walked out the door. Mahogany picked up her notepad and read aloud the poem she had wrote. She titled it Take Care.

'Heartbreak-when it happens it's usually out of the blue, the person least expecting it is left without a clue.

The shocking pain is riveted to the core of your soul, making you believe you can't go on at all.

The hard part of the lesson is finding the strength and courage

To pick up the shattered pieces of your heart.

Who knows? Maybe God had a plan from the beginning... For someone other than the heartbreaker

To take better care of your heart.'

For the first time in her relationship with Damien, Mahogany was unsure as to what step she should take next. Her emotions were stagnant. They had run the gamut on both ends of the spectrum. She wanted to cry and laugh at the same time.

Mahogany put the notepad down and turned out the lights. She was about to get ready for bed when the doorbell rang. Assuming it was Damien she opened the door. Instead she found her none-too-pleased parents.

"I know you have a good excuse for not picking me and your father up from the airport!" demanded Mrs. Fox.

"I know that's right," agreed Mr. Fox.

*   *   *

They were working on borrowed time.

Vladimir Devyatinskiy wiped his brow after listening to President Roy Dean Williams address the United States. He immediately called a presidential meeting with the members of his cabinet. It was only a matter of time before the United States discovered Russia had a heavy hand in the bio-terror attack that hit Washington D.C. Vladimir's hands sweated profusely. If the United States used nuclear warfare on a small country such as Syria, what would they do to his country? He was not going to find out. His country had reelected him as the leader and as the president of Russia and he would not let them down.

Losing the cold war taught Russia one lesson: how to change its strategy. In using the umbrella of democracy versus communism, Russia was given an insurmountable amount of privacy. When Russia covered itself with the shield of communism, every country in the world had a magnifying glass upon her. Yet, when Russia used the shield of democracy, those same countries ignorantly turned a blind eye to her activities. Russia became one of the United States' trusted allies after denouncing communism. Over the years, Russia's deception of democracy systematically persuaded the United States to unilaterally disarm the structure of its defense against Russia. Vladimir watched eagerly from the sidelines as the U.S. diffused early-missile warning systems, grounded strategic bombers, closed dozens of bases, and reduced troop numbers. They were truly disillusioned.

Russia, on the other hand, did the complete opposite. Vladimir made sure that his military continued to build its armory at an unprecedented rate. His navy had over 200 Typhoon class submarines. Submarines, which were silent and undetectable by sonar nets, submarines that had a range of five thousand miles and could reach the United States from Russia's home ports. He fully understood that the best trick in the book was the element of surprise. Now was the time to act on the U.S. vulnerability and resurrect his land to become the superpower it once was. Opportunities such as this only happened once in a lifetime.

Vladimir looked at the two gentlemen, who had stood by his side for the last six years, Gennadiy Devyatinskiy and Bolshoy Andreyevich.

Both men were former generals and sat near the head of the conference table.

"My comrades," started Vladimir, "everyone has a role to play in life and the hour of his or her shining is known only to the universe. Today, I am lucky to tell each one of you that your hour of shining is now. I have given the direct order for a secret attack upon the United States of America. Within a couple of days, the cities, Washington D.C., New York, and Los Angeles will be attacked via nuclear weapons. Our fleets of submarines are already docked at the Caspian Sea waiting for the launch order. Not to mention the submarines we have off the coast of Cuba."

Gennadiy cleared his throat before speaking, "Vladimir are you positive the United States has us within their targets?"

"I have a question for you, Gennadiy. So what if they don't? How can you explain to your fellowmen that you did not seize the opportunity to finally crush the west? The west has silenced our proud banner for the past eighty years. Our ancestors fought for that banner which used to fly so high, past the clouds. We must act decisive and we must act now!" Vladimir pounded his hand on the table, as he spoke, "We will not have a second chance. Those who are ready to ride with me as we retake the reins of power, rise with me. Rise with me!"

With the exception of Gennadiy, all the men at the table slowly rose and began to clap their hands in support. Vladimir looked to his dear friend Gennadiy who finally stood on his feet and declared, "I am with you my friend. The Kremlin shall rise again!"

A new dawn was on the horizon. The sun was about to set on the west.

*　　*　　*

"So how are you holding up?" Mahogany asked. It was the weekend and they finally had a chance to catch up on the events the past week.

"Pretty well, I just picked Chloe up from the baby-sitter's. She was so happy to be home. I'll take her by to see Omar after I get out of the shower. How are things going with your parents?"

Mahogany peeked over her shoulder making sure no one eavesdropped on her phone call.

"They're sleeping. You should have heard them giving me a hard time for not being there to pick them up. My mom had the nerve to tell me that she and my father managed to be there for my birth, the least I could do was remember to pick them up from the airport."

Shanice burst out in laughter, "Your mother is off the hook, Mahogany. Not to change subjects, but do you believe that people reap what they sow?"

"Yes, without a doubt. Why?"

"Well, I finally have my family back together. Granted Omar is in the hospital right now, but I don't believe his illness isn't anything we cannot work through together," hedged Shanice.

"Okay, where is this conversation going? What have you reaped?" wondered Mahogany.

"Yasmine called me while I was at the hospital."

"You are kidding me, Shanice. What did she want?"

"At first she claimed that she was worried about me because she read an article in the newspaper about Omar's attack. However, by the end of our conversation she was whispering sweet-nothings in my ear about missing me and pressuring me to meet her some place. I don't believe she will take no for an answer and I can't risk her reentering my life at this stage," answered Shanice.

"Hmmm, I'm not sure what you can do about her," replied Mahogany. "She's seems unpredictable."

"I seriously wonder, how much longer am I going to pay for my mistake? Is there going to be a moment when I can finally breathe free again? Mahogany, I'm telling you the vibe I got from her is that she will not go away until I see her again."

"Listen, I have an idea. If she wishes to see you again, that's fine. Invite her to church tomorrow night. Tell her it's the only time that you are available to meet and if she refuses to come that's on her. Case closed! Shanice you need to set her straight once and for all and take the initiative. Your marriage is at stake here," finished Mahogany.

"I know you're right. You are acting like I have not tried to convey that to her. I told her it was over when I left that relationship and I told her again when she called."

"Don't wait for her to call," advised Mahogany. "You call her. Put her on notice."

Shanice thought for a moment. Yasmine had her on defense since they broke-up. Maybe it was time for a change in tactics.

"I'll call her right now," declared Shanice. "I'm sick of having butterflies in my stomach every time my telephone rings."

"Handle your business, girl. I'll see you later on tonight at church. Bye-bye."

Shanice did not waste anytime dialing Yasmine. Yasmine answered her phone in a raspy voice.

"Hello."

"Yasmine, this is Shanice…"

"I know the sound of your voice," interrupted Yasmine.

"As I was saying…if you wish to meet up, I will be at the Calvary Fellowship church tomorrow night around 7:00 P.M. I have a lot of things on my plate right now and that is the only time I have available. Is that time a problem for you?"

"No, not at all, what's up with the location?" questioned Yasmine. "There's nothing up. I'm going to be there already and thought I would invite you. If you have a problem meeting at a church then…"

"I don't have a problem, Shanice" responded Yasmine. "It's just a little weird. That's all I'm saying."

"I have become a member of the church." Shanice waited to hear Yasmine's reaction, but it never came.

"Oh, I didn't know. How do you like it?"

"It's pretty nice," answered Shanice. "I've never been a member before so the experience is new to me,"

"That's good to hear. 7:00 P.M. works for me, Shanice. I look forward to seeing you there."

"Okay."

Yasmine hung up the telephone and smiled to herself. She found a crack in Shanice's tough demeanor. Why else would she agree to meet with her? Yasmine knew that both women had a strong connection between them. There were some things people could not deny, no matter how bad they wanted to. If Shanice believed that meeting in a church would hold back the feelings they had for one each other than Yasmine couldn't help but prove her wrong.

*   *   *

"Tell me again why you are going to the building, Mahogany." Mahogany took a deep breath and repeated the same answer that she had given her mother for the past fifteen minutes. Mrs. Fox refused to call a church a "church", she firmly believed that the actual "church" were the people who believed in Jesus Christ and the building was where the church service was held and was nothing more than that—a "building."

"I'm going so I can learn. Tonight is Bible study and I like hearing the Word of God and fellowshipping. You are welcome to come," offered Mahogany.

Mr. Gerald Fox accepted his daughter's offer.

"I thank you for the invitation, baby. Your mother and I would love to pay a visit to your church." He cut his eyes towards his wife, "I mean building," stated Mr. Fox. He didn't know why his wife enjoyed giving their child a hard time about going to church.

"Don't you go speaking on my behalf, Gerald," warned Ms. Fox.

"I can if I want to. I'm your other half and according to the Bible, wives are supposed to obey their husbands." He folded his arms across his chest.

"I'll tell you something husband. Nowhere in the Bible does it say that I must follow a man who isn't following the Lord and if I want to know why my daughter feels the need to sit on a pew, that's my business," replied Mrs. Fox.

"I want you to tell me how I'm not following the Lord," ordered Mr. Fox.

"Do the words "Erk & Jerk" mean anything to you? How about E&J or Ernest and Julio?" quizzed Mrs. Fox.

"Hey! We all know that Jesus turned water into wine. I'm following the Lord because if he didn't want me to drink it, He wouldn't have created it. Now, what do you have to say to that?"

"I don't have anything to say as long as you believe the lie Satan has told you, Gerald."

"Now you want to call me Satan," argued Mr. Fox.

"Mom and Dad, if you're coming with me, please get ready now. I'm going to leave in a half an hour."

"Well, the only reason I'm going is to make sure that you are receiving the correct word," clarified Mrs. Fox. "I consider that to be my duty."

"I consider it my duty to inform you not to make a scene in this church," offered Gerald, "The last church we went to you got us kicked out. Tonya, I'm not up for that tonight. We flew half way across the United States to visit our daughter and I didn't come all this way to get embarrassed by you in a church or building. Understand me?"

Mahogany's father's bald head shone in the light as he gave directives to his wife. He had a valid point in bringing up her mother's last incident inside of a church. When the pastor had asked for an offering, her mom stood up and took it upon herself to declare the minister and his wife lying thieves masquerading as the Lord helpers. Mr. Fox was so humiliated by his wife's behavior, he purchased a wig and mustache to ensure none of his former church members would recognize him.

"You're on thin ice," she warned. "Don't talk to me like I'm your child, Gerald. You think the U.S. is at war now? I'll turn this place into World War III. Keep messing with me."

Mahogany retreated to her bedroom to finish getting dressed. She was happy that her parents were there. They offered her mind a brief reprieve from thinking about Damien. She still did not know what she wanted to do. Should she move on in her life or should she try to see his side of the story? She finished putting Lucas's church outfit on and grabbed her car keys.

It began to rain. Although, they were fifteen minutes behind schedule, the ride to the church was an uneventful one. Mrs. Fox found an urban radio station to lighten the mood inside the car. She even took the liberty of rapping to a DMX song until they got to the church. After the arrival, Mrs. Fox commented on the large amount of people who entered the building.

"My goodness, Mahogany, your Pastor must be real popular if he can get people to turn out to see him in weather like this. I can't wait to hear him speak."

The choir sang *Awesome God* as the ushers directed them to their seats. Mahogany was mildly surprised when she noticed Yasmine sitting next to Shanice, for a moment she second guessed if she gave Shanice the correct advice by inviting Yasmine. Once the choir finished singing, Pastor Ethan led them in prayer and began his sermon.

"Good evening, good evening. I'm happy to see everyone made it here safely," mentioned Pastor Ethan, "For tonight, I have a special word to share. How many of you are familiar with the saying 'knowledge is power?'" Hands flew up throughout the building. He continued, "The

Lord told his prophet Hosea, 'My people are destroyed for lack of knowledge."

"Amen, Amen, Pastor preach!" the congregation ordered.

"We last left off in 1st John 12:31 I discussed how Satan is described in the Bible as the ruler of the world which we live in. This chapter plainly tells us that the whole world lies under the sway of Satan. As Christians, we are literally standing on a battleground. We reside on Satan's home turf, but remember, that greater is He that is in us than he who is in the world. The victory over the flesh is to be what?" Pastor Ethan questioned the congregation.

"Led by the Holy Spirit," his flock responded.

"I can't hear you. Victory over the flesh is what?!" he shouted. "To be led by the Holy Spirit!" the congregation yelled.

"That's right, walk in the Spirit, and you shall not fulfill the lust of the flesh!"

"Amen, Amen!" Everyone stood on their feet in approval.

"Turn to Ephesians 6:10. Paul instructs us to put on the whole armor of God for the battle we are facing. The sword of the Spirit, which is the word of God.' We must continually stand firm in faith and strong in the Word of God. Please understand your adversary, the devil!" Pastor Ethan used a handkerchief to wipe his sweat-drenched forehead.

"How many of you have prayed and prayed and have never received an answer? All of us know that when we ask the Lord for anything it is crucial that we BELIEVE that we already have it. When Satan attacks our thoughts, we start to doubt ourselves and the Lord, which leads to a lack of faith. We must keep our faith! Oh, I don't think you're hearing me tonight!"

Mahogany stood up alongside her parents as they clapped their hands. Mrs. Fox lifted her hands above her head and yelled, "Glory! Glory be to God!" as Pastor Ethan continued.

"We are to hold on to our faith with every fiber of our being. Our soul and spirit needs that nourishment. Our soul can live for an eternity. The question I have for each and every one of you is: Do you know where your soul will go once you depart from this earth? I'm asking you to take a chance on Christ. He will never, never, never leave you. Who do you know in your life that can make a promise to you such as that? If you don't know anyone, please come down the aisle so that you may get to know a man named Jesus. Tomorrow is not guaranteed to anyone," finished Pastor Ethan.

Rising in their royal blue robes, the choir began to sing the song, *Tomorrow*, a touching song written by the Winans'.

Jesus said,

"Here I stand, won't you please let me in?" And you said,

"I will tomorrow"

Jesus said,

"I am He who supplies all your needs" And you said,

"I know, but tomorrow, oh, tomorrow, I'll give my life

Tomorrow, I thought about today, but it's so much easier to say"

Tomorrow, who promised you tomorrow? Better choose the Lord today, for Tomorrow very well might be too late.

Yasmine stood to her feet. Many of the words spoken tonight cut to her heart. She couldn't describe the feeling coursing throughout her body. All she knew was that it was an authentic emotion. Real enough to draw her from her pew and towards the pulpit. But before she could take her first step, embarrassment and an overwhelming sense of guilt flooded her body. She felt naked standing in front of everyone. Instead of going down to the pulpit, Yasmine hurriedly ran outside the doors and into the pouring rain. The rain beat down upon her face intermingling with her tears. The choir's song still reached her ears as she stood outside.

Jesus said,

"Here I stand, won't you please take my hand?" And you said,

"I will tomorrow"

Jesus said,

"I am he who supplies all your needs" And you said,

"I know, but tomorrow, oh, tomorrow, I'll give my life

Tomorrow, I thought about today, Oh, but it's so much easier to say"

Holding her head up to the sky, Yasmine turned to go back inside the church. Sadly, at the last moment, she changed her mind and walked to her car with the final words of the song running through her mind.

And who said tomorrow would ever come for you Still you laugh and play and continue on to say... Tomorrow, forget about tomorrow won't you give

Your life today, oh,

Please don't just turn and walk away

Tomorrow, tomorrow...

Don't let this moment slip away

Your tomorrow could very well begin today.

Chapter Seven

Dawn dialed the telephone number with a trembling hand. She and Trent agreed to call Nina Fitzgerald first thing in the morning. It was all she could do not to chew off all her fingernails and literally climb the walls last night. She slept a total of two hours during the past twenty- four hours. She would never admit it, but she was happy that Trent stayed with her. The new structure of their relationship reinforced Dawn's belief that every thought and action happened for a reason. She knew that neither of them were ready to raise a child when their son was born. Yet now, years later, they were desperately trying to find him so that they may offer him their love. A love that both were too selfish to give at a time when their son needed it most. Dawn was extremely grateful for the love the Fitzgerald's showed Nathaniel.

"It's ringing," Dawn whispered to Trent and he grabbed her other hand for support.

"We're sorry the telephone number you dialed has been disconnected. Please check the number you are calling and try your call again. Area code, two zero eight."

"Trent, it's disconnected," Dawn said dejectedly, "What can that possibly mean? My brain will start to melt if I begin to think of all the reasons her telephone is disconnected. Do you think it's because she could no longer work and couldn't afford a phone bill? Or…" He could read her eyes. She was thinking worst case scenario.

"Listen, to me. We do not know why the phone is disconnected, so what is the purpose of worrying about it? All we can do is stay on track to find our son. Our journey doesn't end over one disconnected phone line. She could have forgotten to pay the telephone bill, Dawn. We honestly don't know."

"You're right," She noticed that he still held her hand and she slowly removed it from his grasp. "We'll find him. I believe that." Dawn ran her fingers through her hair. "What's the next move," she whispered to herself. "We have the telephone number, why don't I ask Lt. Peck to go to Google and type in the telephone number in the search box then we can figure out the location."

"That's a great idea! Let's do it," agreed Trent.

"Okay, it's about lunch time in North Carolina. Lt. Peck should be at his desk, stuffing a Barbecue Lodge pork sandwich down his throat," Dawn theorized as she dialed his office number.

"Hello?" said a muffled voice.

"Peck, this is Dawn. I trust that I am interrupting your delicious lunch?" she asked.

"You must have your radar on. I just took a bite out of my sandwich. You better have a good reason for disturbing me, Ms. Price," he joked.

"Well, I do,"

Dawn tried to contain the excitement in her voice as she spoke to him, but it was difficult to do. In more ways than one, Lt. Peck provided a shelter from the daily battles Dawn willingly put herself through to find her son. It wasn't an easy task of getting her hopes up on every tip that she managed to dig up. Dawn filled him in on the details surrounding the disconnected number.

"That should be simple enough to do," Lt. Peck stated, "What is the telephone number?"

"It's 208-555-5791."

"Hold on a sec' while I type this in." Dawn could hear his fingers pecking in the background. "I got it. The telephone number belongs to a Mrs. Bernice Carson and the physical address is 8011 Elm Street in Boise, Idaho."

"That's fantastic news since we're not too far from there. I know exactly where it is."

"Good, that means I won't have to give you directions."

"Does it show anything else? I'm trying to figure out why Nina wrote down Bernice Carson's address. I guess we will figure it out when we get there."

"I guess you will," Lt. Peck replied, "Now, if you won't need my services anymore, I'm gonna get back to my sandwich. Let me know how everything pans out."

"I will," promised Dawn. She hung up the phone and turned to

Trent. "Jackpot!" she yelled. "What did he say?"

"We have the address. 8011 Elm Street is the location of the telephone number. Let's go," she urged.

"Are you for real? He found it? Just that quick?" Trent asked. He was incredulous, technology was something else.

"Indeed he did," Dawn smiled. "Hand me your keys, I'll drive," she offered.

If memory served her correctly, Elm Street was less than ten minutes away from the hotel. Trying to stay below the speed limit was the main challenge, her right foot acted like it had a mind of its own. Trent tried to ease the nervousness by telling a joke.

"Have you heard the joke about the guy that went to a doctor?" "No," hedged Dawn, "I can't say that I have."

"Well, one day this guy went to the doctor and the doctor says to him: Sir, you have a banana in your ear and the guy says, "What?" then the doctor tells him again, 'Sir, you have a banana in your ear. Then the guy turns to the doctor and yells, "What? I can't hear you. I have a banana in my ear." Dawn gave a warm giggle.

"Is that the best one you had?" she questioned.

"Yea, it is. It's the only joke I could think of at a time like this. I tried bringing a little levity to the situation. Did it work?"

"It worked a little bit. My heart is still racing a mile a minute though."

"So is mine," admitted Trent, "So is mine." Both were quiet until the car came to a stop at 8011 Elm Street.

The red and gray house marked 8011 appeared vacant. There were no curtains in any of the windows and old newspapers lined the driveway. Although the house was empty, the well-manicured lawn gave the tale-tale sign of an upper class suburb. Images of little Nate running through the yard flooded Dawn's mind. From the stacks of newspapers, it appeared the house had been unoccupied for several months.

"Another dead end, why am I not surprised?" mocked Dawn. "You have no idea how much I hate my mother right now, Trent."

"I know, but hate is a strong word to throw around, Dawn."

"I don't care, Trent. That woman who claims to be my mother has caused me more personal pain than any other person in this entire world. How can she show such contempt for me? Do you think that Nate feels the same way about me? After all, I gave him away like I didn't care about him." Trent grabbed her by the shoulders and forced her to look into his eyes.

"Don't you dare say that! You are nothing like that shell of person called your mother. Your mother's blood runs cold as ice and you are the complete opposite. If you were like your mother, you would not give a damn about your son! So don't sit here and try to start a pity party because you will be the only one in attendance. Understand?"

"I understand. It's just that I'm so tired. My emotions have been stretched to the max and for what? For my feelings to get crushed time after time…"

"Dawn, I thought I told you that I was not attending this pity party. You know what my mother used to tell me? God would never put on you more than you could bare. I believed her. Do you think we came all this way for nothing?" Trent watched her shake her head.

"No."

"All we have to do is find the next piece of the puzzle. Simple as that. What's your next plan of action?"

"I'm not sure," Dawn said quietly, "You tell me since you refused to come to my party."

"First thing we need to do is find out who this Bernice Carson is and see how she connects to Nina. I know someone at the police station who may be able to help us."

"Alright," voiced Dawn. She tried to sound optimistic, but Trent could tell she was folding from the stress. "I didn't know that you had a connection."

"Hand me the car keys," ordered Trent. "She should be there right now."

"Don't you think we should call first before we just show up?"

"Nah, she wouldn't mind. We're old buddies," answered Trent. He could tell that Dawn wanted more information. "We were old drinking buddies, if you must know."

"I didn't say anything," she smirked.

"I know, but I could read your eyes. You didn't have to say a word," Trent opened the passenger side door for her and got in on the other side. He almost had the key in the ignition before Dawn's question stopped him in his tracks.

"Did you mean platonic drinking buddies?" A strong grin spread across Trent's face before he answered Dawn's question.

"I didn't say did I?" he joked. "Karefina and I are just friends. We met each other at A.A. and both of us managed to stay on the wagon at the same time. Trust me, she's good peeps."

"Karefina? What kind of name is 'Karefina'?"

"Dawn, do I detect a hint of jealousy in your voice?"

"No, there isn't. I just didn't want to have any awkward moments, that's all. You know some people have a history, and if they believe that someone else is infringing on their history, things can get ugly and…"

"Dawn, you are babbling."

"I'm babbling," she confessed.

"Although, I would love to listen to more of your insightfulness regarding history infringements, I think its best that we leave now." He truly enjoyed watching her squirm.

"I agree." Dawn hoped that her face wasn't a bright shade of red. She purposely made an effort to keep her lips sealed until they arrived at the Boise Police Station.

Dawn stood in the background when Trent spoke with the desk clerk.

"Yes, I need to see Karefina Vincent." "Is she expecting you sir?"

"No, she isn't. Please tell her that Trent Royal is here to see her." A few minutes passed before Trent recognized Karefina's familiar face coming towards him. She gave him an old fashion bear hug.

"Trent! I could not believe my ears when they told me you were out here. Goodness gracious, how long has it been since we last saw each other?"

"Six or seven months? I can't remember."

"Turn around, let me see how you are coming along, sugar."

Dawn stood in silence as Trent did an obligatory pirouette. Karefina appeared to be in her late forties and in perfect shape. She sported a mini-afro that would give Maya Angelo a run for her money.

"I see you are taking good care of yourself. It seems like you've gained a few muscles. Now tell me, who is this pretty little thing standing next to you?"

"This is Dawn," he informed Karefina.

After the introductions, Karefina took them back to her office where

Trent explained his situation to her. "What do you need me to do?"

"Please check in your database to see if there is anything you can find on Bernice Carson or Nina Fitzgerald?"

"I can get into a lot of trouble doing this, but I'll do whatever I can to help," Karefina emitted a gruff laugh, "Hey, you only live once, so why not make a big difference in someone's life?"

"Karefina, I hate to put you in such a precarious situation, but our back is up against the wall and we need some answers. I do appreciate you going out on a limb for us."

"So do I," echoed Dawn.

"Just hold your thanks until I give you something to be thankful for," Karefina commented.

Trent and Dawn waited patiently while she gathered all the information. There were several moments when she had to leave the office for long periods of time. The final time she came back into the office, Trent could read the anxiety in her body language.

"I'm not sure how to tell you this, but I have found some of the answers you were looking for and have some news that is a bit disturbing. Nina Fitzgerald died four months ago."

"Oh my," said Trent.

"Bernice Carson was her best friend and according to the EMT report. Nina Fitzgerald passed away at Bernice's house which is 8011 Elm Street."

"What about Nathaniel? Where is he?" Dawn inquired. She watched at Karefina exhale a long, deep breath.

"For whatever reason, Bernice was unable to keep Nathaniel and called social services to find a family for him. He was placed in a foster care home owned by a lady named Monique Tate. Unbeknownst to us, Ms. Tate's current live in boyfriend, Leon Mathers, had an arrest warrant for drug possession and an attempted murder charge. When the police finally nailed down his location, Monique and Leon decided to leave town, taking Nathaniel with them. I'm so sorry." Trent slammed his hand down on the desk in disbelief.

"This is too much. You are telling us that the only mother that our son has ever known is dead, and oh, by the way, he's on the lam with a known felon?"

"Trent, wait, there's more. When the police officers questioned the Tate's neighbors for possible leads, we learned some distressing information. Not only did the neighbors not provide any useful information; they claimed to hear sounds of abuse from the household. Some alleged that Ms. Tate only brought children into the household for the extra money from the state."

"That's just great, really great! I can't...," said Trent.

"We understand and are trying to do everything we can to find them," assured Karefina.

Dawn had a hard time following the conversation. She felt so hot and stuffy. Every word Karefina spoke seemed to fade further away. Dawn looked towards Trent as the room slowly spun out of control.

The last thing she saw before losing consciousness were Trent arms reaching out for her as she hit the floor.

*   *   *

Damien took special care in getting dressed. Tonight was a very special evening that required every little detail to be perfect. His pants and shirt were ironed to a crisp. He neatly straightened his Ralph Lauren tie around his neck. Looking in the mirror, he realized that the reflection staring back at him was from a different man he had known for the past twenty-eight years or, shall we say, from the last couple of weeks. He was ready to claim the woman who captured his heart. After trimming his goatee, Damien put his cuff links on, and slipped into his suit jacket. He grabbed the keys to his car and left out the door.

Damien spoke with Mrs. Fox earlier in the day. He learned that tonight Mahogany and her family would spend their evening at church. His nerves tried to get the best of him as he drove to his destination. He rubbed the little box in his front pocket. No way would he let her leave his life. It was an established fact that they shared a wonderful child together, but he needed her as his confidant and lover as well.

Mahogany didn't know he stopped by to visit her parents nor that he paid a visit to Pastor Ethan. Taking advantage of her father being in town, Damien asked Mr. Fox for his daughter's hand in marriage. Mr. Fox only had a few comments, "You hurt her, and I'll kill you. Simple as that, do you understand what I am telling you? Because I don't want to cross this bridge again." The meeting with Pastor Ethan happened to be more promising.

Yesterday after work, he passed by the church hoping to see Mahogany's car there. When he didn't see it, on a whim he decided to go inside to discuss with Pastor Ethan his future plans with Mahogany. From the moment Damien stepped foot in his office, Pastor Ethan had the ability to discern and read Damien like a book. It was an unnerving experience.

"Have a seat, please. I'm sorry if I forgot your name."

"It's Damien." Pastor Ethan shook his hand then sat down behind his desk.

"What can I do for you today?"

"I honestly don't know. I really didn't plan on stopping by, but then I decided to come in and share with you my plans to marry Mahogany. I know that she thinks very highly of you." Mahogany told Damien the interesting discussions she had with Pastor Ethan.

"Well, congratulations! That's great! She seems to be a very fine young lady. You are a very blessed man," he commented. "So when is the big day?"

"Well, I haven't asked her yet," confessed Damien, "I was hoping that you could offer me some advice and that you would do us the honor of performing the ceremony."

"First let me ask you a couple of questions. Are you a believer in Christ?"

"Yes, I am," answered Damien.

"Well, that answer sounded like it came straight from an old Sunday school class. How often do you read your Bible?"

Damien thought about it for a moment. He could not recall the last time he picked up a Bible. He took a religion class in college which required him to purchase a Bible and that was over ten years ago.

"Honestly, I do not have a Bible," he nervously cleared his throat, "and as far as a relationship, I believe that I have one."

"Do you call on Him in a time of need?"

"No."

"Damien, I'm going to give you some advice. I sense you are unsure about your commitment to the Lord. In my opinion, once you get serious and develop a relationship with Christ, the battles and obstacles you fight will only get easier."

Damien allowed Pastor Ethan's words to settle in his mind before he spoke.

"I understand," Damien stood up to leave, "Thanks for listening to me."

"No problem, I want to invite you to service tomorrow," said Pastor Ethan.

"Thank you, I'll be here." Damien shook his hand.

"Godspeed with your marriage proposal, let me know how everything goes, Damien."

That discussion took place forty eight hours ago. When he was within five miles of the church, he eased his foot off the gas. Damien replayed every single line he would say to Mahogany in his head. He prayed that she would say yes, but, he could not blame her if she did not. Once he arrived at the destination, he turned the ignition off and began his walk inside. Damien inconspicuously found a seat in the rear of the church. Pastor Ethan had finished his sermon.

Damien spotted Mahogany sitting at the end of the aisle with her parents before he strode boldly to the pulpit. Pastor Ethan immediately acknowledged him with a beaming smile and hug.

"I have something else I need to say," Damien turned around and faced the crowd. He immediately found Mahogany. "I also wish to rededicate my life to you especially if you let me. This woman is my friend and the mother of my child and has been with me through thick and thin. When I think about the horrible things I've done to her in the past, it rips me apart because she has been nothing less than an angel to me. And sometimes," Damien paused a moment before he continued. "Sometimes

I unintentionally crushed your wings and I'm sorry for that. I love you with every fiber of my being." Damien pulled a blue jewelry box from his pocket and knelt on one knee. "Mahogany Fox, will you do me the honor of becoming my wife? Will you marry me?"

She was shocked to see Damien walking down to the pulpit and made up her mind about her future with Damien. The fact that she had taken so long to make a decision about their relationship offered a clue. She cared for him. Before answering his question, she asked herself if she would live to regret her answer. Deep down she knew that she wouldn't. She remembered all of the times she hoped and prayed that he would change and stop playing around. Grabbing his face, she kissed him.

"Yes, yes, I will," Mahogany responded in a loud voice.

*   *   *

Pope David Ibraham sat in the holy chair caressing his rosaries. He was meditating.

"Today is the day that she will make her magnificent appearance to all," he said to himself.

An hour hadn't passed before the Vatican's phone line began ringing off the hook. Every priest, bishop, and cardinal from around the globe called describing apparitions of the Blessed Mother. It never ceased to amaze David how emotional people were after claiming they saw the apparition. From the beginning of time, the apparitions of Mary were intended to convey that Mary still had the superior position in her relationship with his adversary, the Christ.

David went out to the papal balcony where throngs of millions had gathered outside the Vatican to see the most beautiful apparition. The Blessed Mother Mary was enveloped within a bright radiant light as exquisite clouds surrounded her in the background.

David joined the crowd in giving a thunderous round of applause. He waited until the applause stopped before finally speaking.

"In practicing what our Blessed Mother has taught us, I would like to take this moment to extend an olive branch to our Jewish brothers. This is not the time for our Muslims brothers to mourn for the destruction of the Al-Aqsa. It is time to extend our hand in friendship and kindness to the Jews. The Vatican has chosen to return the ancient artifacts of the Jewish Temple to our friends in Israel. If they chose to rebuild a temple for their God, who are we to judge? Muslims have gained so much faith and love from the Al-Aqsa, it's time that we returned the same gesture."

The apparition hovered above the crowd with her arms out-stretched. Immediately, the thousands of people below fell to their knees to bow and worship; they could not believe their eyes.

Chapter Eight

Mahogany breathlessly scrambled for her telephone through the piles of wedding magazines on her bed.

"Hello? Hello?"

"Hi Mahogany, its Dawn."

"Dawn, I think I recognize your voice by now," Mahogany replied, "I'm happy you called. You are not going to believe what I'm doing tomorrow."

"What?" Dawn questioned. Knowing Mahogany, it could be anything.

"I'm getting married! Can you believe it?" yelled Mahogany.

"No way!" shouted Dawn, "Congratulations, I'm really happy for you. I will have to get the details later, but the lucky guy is Damien I presume?"

"That is correct," confirmed Mahogany.

"Well, I hate to rain on your parade but I'm calling for a favor."

"Sure. Are you okay?" Mahogany could hear the hesitation in her voice.

"Honestly, no, I'm not. That's why I'm calling you. I'm feel as though I'm about to lose my mind, Mahogany and I don't know where else to turn."

"Tell me what happened."

"I can't," Dawn said honestly, "or it will release the flood gates. This is the first time today that I have been able to talk without bursting into tears. Please, just listen to me, Mahogany. Can you pray for the safe return of my son? It's just that I have nowhere else to go and I have done all that I can do."

Dawn's trepidation was tangible through the telephone. Mahogany wanted to provide her with comfort.

"Oh, Dawn, you know that you don't have to ask. I would love to pray with you," Mahogany closed her eyes and spoke aloud, "Father, we boldly come to You today to ask for the safe return of Dawn's son. You said in your word, "Ask and you shall receive." We believed it then and we definitely believe it now. Father, we do believe that this child will be safely returned to his mother. We know all things are possible through Christ and wish to thank you for hearing our prayers and answering them, in Jesus name, Amen."

"Amen," Dawn said in low voice.

"Thanks Mahogany. I've gotta run. I'll talk to you later." "Bye."

Mahogany hung up the telephone. She could only imagine the living torture that Dawn had put herself through in searching for her son. It was a small price to pay. The love of a mother was a very powerful emotion.

*   *   *

Omar sat in his hospital bed captivated by the television. He watched as news reporters from around the world provided coverage regarding the Marian visions.

"Honey, have you seen this? I still can't figure out how they put those invisible wires on her outfit," commented Omar. "She's floating around."

"Neither can I," confessed Shanice, "The scary thing about the whole thing is that I believe there weren't any wires. Over a hundred different camera angles got the exact pictures of the Pope and the apparition. She was actually flying through the air. This world is changing and I don't think it's for the better."

"I know. What causes me alarm is how every single reporter referred to Jesus as the son of Mary versus the Son of God. Call me crazy, but it seems like there is a hidden agenda lurking beneath all this hoopla. What are you thinking about? I can see that deep furrow between your eyes."

"I'm worried about you. I feel so helpless watching you suffer and I have these thoughts come to my mind imaging the worse. Then I worry about Chloe…"

"Shanice, I understand what you are saying, but will worrying about it solve anything?"

"Well, no," whispered Shanice.

"What has Mahogany been up to? I haven't seen her around lately?" Shanice laughed before answering his question.

"You'll never guess," she teased.

"Oh this must be really good," he rubbed his hands together gleefully, "I'm going to say that she has found a good man to keep her occupied," Omar guessed.

"That's pretty close," said Shanice, "Well, drum roll please…Mahogany and Damien have decided to tie the knot."

"Get out! No way! When?" Omar demanded.

"Let's see. I spoke with Mahogany today and she and Damien are getting married um, hmm, what did she say? Tomorrow!!! They're getting married tomorrow!!"

"What? When did they start seeing each other again? I had no idea." Omar appeared genuinely surprised.

"They have been off and on during the last couple of months, but this last week they got pretty serious. He proposed to her last night and, since her parents are already in town, they decided to get married since her family is already here. They did not want to wait any longer. I'm so happy for her. From the way she sounded, Damien really has gotten his act together."

"When were you going to tell me? That's huge news to be holding in.," admitted Omar.

"I wanted to wait and see what the doctors said about how soon you could leave the hospital. I know you are going crazy not being able to track the U.S. led war in Syria or following up with your leads about the impending Russian attack. I just didn't want to add anything else to your list."

"Thanks for being concerned, but I don't think attending a wedding will finish me off. What time tomorrow?"

"It will be at 3:00 P.M. I'm supposed to be the Matron of Honor," Shanice added. "I have to wear this flowery yellow dress she picked out for me." Omar's expression turned serious.

"I remember the day when you wore a white dress for me. I know things got a little rough in the past, but I want to take this time to sincerely tell you thank you."

"Well," said Shanice. She fanned her eyes to stop herself from crying, "I'm not an easy woman to get rid of, Mr. Miller."

"I know, baby. Boy, do I know!" he joked.

"I have only one thing to say: You're more than welcome," she said then kissed him passionately. For the first time since Omar's diagnoses, she allowed herself to fully relax and not be troubled about what may come next. After all, what could ever be accomplished from worrying?

*   *   *

Today was her wedding day. If it weren't for her mother primping over every little detail from her hair to her make-up, Mahogany would not believe it. Her mother and Lucas were alone in the bridal room. They had been up since six o'clock that morning and in less than fifteen minutes she would be known as Mrs. Mahogany Andrews. Pastor Ethan would be the minister to pronounce her and Damien husband and wife. He made a rare exception provided the short notice given to him.

"Mahogany, it seems everyone is ready for you," said Mrs. Fox. "Mama, this is really happening isn't it?"

"Yes it is, baby," replied Mrs. Fox.

"Where's dad?" inquired Mahogany.

"He is waiting outside this door ready to walk you down the aisle. Now are you ready girl or what?" Mahogany stood up from out her chair.

"I'm ready. I'm ready to become a married woman now," smiled Mahogany.

Mrs. Fox looked over her daughter standing before her wearing a simple, yet elegant white wedding dress. The longer Mrs. Fox stared at her, the more emotional she felt.

"Girl, if you make me cry and mess up my make-up I'm going to hurt you," sighed Mrs. Fox.

Mahogany could have sworn that she saw a drop of water emerge from the corner of her mother's eye, but it was wiped away before Mahogany could confirm it. A knock on the door allowed the moment to pass before either had a chance to say anything.

"That's probably your father," mentioned Mrs. Fox, "I'm going to take my seat. But before I do, I feel as though I need to tell you something. I'm proud of you and my grandson, Lucas. From what I see, Damien has come a long way and the place he is right now is just right. Because we tend to want the very best for our children, every mother dreams of an unflawed man for their daughter. The way Damien looks at you…sometimes I wish your father would look at me the same way, if only for five minutes. You've done well, baby. I love you." Mahogany gave her mother a big bear hug.

"I love you, too," murmured Mahogany. She heard her father open the door.

"Tonya, what do you mean that I don't look at you in that way? I heard what you told our daughter," he accused. "How about if you look at me in that special kind of way? I've been looking at you the same way for the past twenty years, now all of sudden, it's a problem," complained Mr. Fox.

"Gerald, we can discuss this at a different time," promised Mrs. Fox, "And for the record, I did not say that it was a problem. If you are going to eavesdrop, then do it correctly. I hear the music playing, I better take my seat."

"I know that's right," said Mr. Fox after playfully swatting Mrs. Fox on her behind before she left the room. "Tonight, I'll look at you in that special kind of way. I guarantee it," he finished. "I hear your song playing, Sunshine. I want to tell you that you will always be my baby girl."

After pulling the veil over her face, Mahogany's father kissed her hand and led her down the aisle. As they walked down the aisle, Mahogany was extremely surprised to see her extended family. Her sisters, Tasha, Maisa, her Aunt Irlean, Aunt Evelyn, Uncle Rodney, Cousin Theresa, and other members of her family were present, many of whom she hadn't seen in years. Yet, her astonishment faded when she saw Damien standing at the end of the aisle. He was a vision straight out of a romance novel. His dark wavy hair caressed each feature of his face as his trimmed sideburns added an ingredient of sexiness that only Damien could possess. Shivers went down Mahogany's spine the closer she got to him. Without question, his looks were stunning. For a moment time stood still.

"Who gives this woman away?" questioned Pastor Ethan.

"I do," responded Mr. Fox, then he sat in his designated seat.

Once Pastor Ethan started the ceremony, Mahogany gradually tuned everything out. She allowed each word he spoke to sew a seed inside her heart. When the time came to exchange their vows, Mahogany lost her composure when Damien spoke his personal marriage vows aloud.

"I, Damien, take you Mahogany to be my lawfully wedded wife. You are my life-long companion and my soul mate. For richer or poorer, I will not leave your side. If you become ill, I would willingly give my own life so that you may have yours. Not even death can separate the love my soul has for you. So I cannot truthfully say "till death do us part" because I believe our love is the kind of love that transcends time. I give you this ring as a symbol of my unyielding devotion to you." Damien placed the four carat diamond upon Mahogany's finger.

"I love you," she tearfully whispered.

When it was her turn to say her vows, Mahogany repeated the customary vows spoken aloud by Pastor Ethan. She was positive that everyone within the church could hear the nervousness in her voice, but she didn't care. The only item of concern for her was the last sentence stated by Pastor Ethan.

"By the power vested in me by the state of North Carolina, I now pronounce you husband and wife. You may kiss your bride."

Damien placed the veil on top of her head and gently grabbed her face between his hands and planted a soft, passionate kiss on her lips.

"Ladies and Gentlemen: May I present to you, Mr. and Mrs. Damien Andrews," shouted Pastor Ethan.

Shanice watched Damien immediately take hold of Mahogany's hand. From her perspective, it seemed like he would never let go. As her eyes followed Mahogany through the crowd, Shanice was surprised when she spotted Yasmine near the front door of the church. Working her way through the crowd, Shanice caught up with Yasmine before she left.

"Hey, I didn't know you were going to be here," mentioned Shanice. "Yea, neither did I. Mahogany called and invited me. I didn't know until this morning if I would actually attend," Yasmine confessed, "You look really nice, Shanice." Yasmine observed an uneasiness pass over Shanice's face. "No, I didn't mean it like that. I was just saying in general. I'm sorry. Well, it was nice seeing you."

"I haven't heard from you since the night I invited you to church. I wondered if everything was okay."

"Yea, it's good. My life was changed that night—not instantaneously, but nevertheless, changed. It forced me to think about my life and speculate if the choices I've made were right. I guess what really bothered me is that the Pastor made me doubt myself. That was the strangest part and I'm still working on that aspect."

"I see," replied Shanice. "Are you going to the reception?"

"No, somehow I don't believe your husband would be too crazy about that. But thanks for the offer, Shanice. I'll be seeing you around."

"Bye, Yasmine. Take care," said Shanice.

"Thank you," said Yasmine.

Watching her walk out the door, Shanice knew deep down that she would probably never hear from Yasmine again. It was true that some people were in one's life for only a season. No doubt, Yasmine finally understood the season they once shared was over.

Omar came up from behind and planted a kiss on the nape of her neck.

"Have you been trying to hide from me? The only way I could find you was by following all the stares of the men looking at you."

"Oh really? Where are they?" she teased.

"Very funny. Wasn't that a lovely ceremony?" asked Omar. "It was a beautiful one. Maybe we should do it again?"

"If you're asking me to marry you, then the answer is yes," Omar felt the vibration of his cell phone ringing. "Could be a hot lead," he said before answering his phone.

"Omar, this is Dawn. I'm sorry to be calling you on your phone, but I'm trying to reach Mahogany. I know this is her wedding day and I wouldn't be calling her if it wasn't important."

"Who is it?" mouthed Shanice.

Omar covered the mouthpiece of the telephone and whispered to

Shanice that is was Dawn.

"She really needs to speak with Mahogany. I think it's an emergency."

Shanice grabbed Omar's telephone and went in search of Mahogany. Shanice found her standing outside the church posing for the photographer. Shanice had to pause for a second and watch her. She and Mahogany were finally grown-up. Gone were their days of practical jokes, Color Purple skits, and heart wrenching sob stories of love. They had come a long way from Boise, Idaho. Shanice waited for the photographer to finish before approaching Mahogany.

"Mahogany, Dawn is on the phone, she really needs to speak with you," said Shanice.

"Dawn? Is everything okay?"

"It is! That is why I am calling you. I had to speak with you. First, how did your wedding go? I can hear all the partiers in the background."

"Oh Dawn, I wish you could have been here. Everything was so perfect! I could not have asked for a better wedding. I feel like Cinderella at the ball. But enough about me. Tell me what happened."

"Mahogany, not even an hour had passed after I hung up the telephone with you before Trent came rushing into my room. He was talking so fast that I could not understand him. When he finally able to say a full sentence, he said the words I will never forget, "They found him!" Mahogany, did you hear me?! They found my baby! His named is Nathaniel."

"Really, Dawn. To say that it's wonderful would be an understatement. It is truly a blessing. I'm so happy for you. Where was he?" questioned Mahogany.

"To make a long story short, it was nothing short of a miracle. I know I haven't filled you in on a lot of the details, but Nate's foster mother, Monique, was pretty roughed up by her boyfriend. When she went to the hospital for help, the hospital notified the authorities, and when the authorities showed up, little Nate was there with her. The authorities dropped a line to our contact, Karefina, and we left that night to drive to Pocatello where they were. Oh, Mahogany, you should see him."

"What did Trent say?"

"Mahogany, I think he's cried more than I have. After I told him how we prayed, he said, there is no way a person can believe that there is no God. That is why I'm calling you, to tell you that I do believe in God. You see, I never witnessed such a miracle like this before, how God made a way out of no way. Thank you. Each time I look into the eyes of my son, I am reminded of God and how He answered my prayers. The first time I saw him, it was like he recognized me, maybe. I'm just hoping, but to me it seemed real. He looks so much like Trent. I'm watching the two of them together right now and its love. That's the only way I can describe it."

"How are things between you two?" hinted Mahogany. Damien began kissing Mahogany's arm.

"We're good. Actually we decided to give it another go round. I don't know if he is going to move down there or if I'm going to move up here. I don't think Idaho is a place I would want to live again. I'm going to let you go. I know that you're busy and just wanted to catch you before your honeymoon. Bye."

"Bye, Dawn. Be sure to give him a great, big kiss for me. I can't wait to see him," replied Mahogany. She handed the cell phone back to Shanice.

"She found her son didn't she?"

"Not only did she find her son, she also discovered that, God will be there for us every time."

"I know that's right!" shouted Mr. Fox. "Now can we break out the E&J and get this party started?"

"I know he didn't say that at my baby's wedding," yelled Mrs. Fox. Mahogany watched in amusement as her parents continued their shenanigans. Some things never changed, she assumed. Damien picked Lucas up and wrapped his other arm around her waist as the photographer took their picture. Smiling into the camera, Mahogany wished that the camera lens was able to capture the love that bonded them.

Chapter Nine

The following day Shanice waited in Omar's hospital room for the test results. She hoped the news Dr. Rafti shared would be positive for a change. Chloe sat in a nearby chair doodling in her coloring book. Shanice heard familiar squeaks of Omar's wheelchair before he entered the room. From the look on Dr. Rafti's face, Shanice could tell that the news was troubling.

"Omar?" she said.

He cleared his throat before speaking.

"Baby, I have some bad news. I need to begin chemotherapy immediately," he stated, but Dr. Rafti interrupted him before he could finish.

"Mrs. Miller, the cancer is more advanced than the test showed. I want you to know that we will use a regiment that is top of line in battling this disease," promised Dr. Rafti. "Your husband is in great shape and…"

As Dr. Rafti spoke, Omar, Shanice, and Chloe looked at the ceiling. They both heard a loud trumpet sound and in a twinkling of an eye all three were gone. Dr. Rafti froze and fear paralyzed him when he saw the clothes of the Miller family fall to the floor.

*   *   *

In an effort to steal more of his body heat, Mahogany snuggled closer to Damien. As she gathered the comforter around her, she heard the most peculiar sound. The only way to describe it was that the reverberation reminded her of someone blowing a horn. The sound was deafening to her ears. Damien hearing the noise awoke with a start and held tight to Mahogany as they both disappeared.

*   *   *

Pastor Ethan's home phone rang as he was leaving his house. He debated answering it before picking up the telephone.

"Hello?"

"Hi Pastor, this is Joshua. I didn't wake you did I?"

"No, I was just heading out the door. I had a lot of errands to run today," he replied.

"Well, I'm a little embarrassed to be calling you, but I needed to know how the wedding ceremony went," Joshua admitted, "I couldn't bear to be there."

"Everything went perfectly fine, Joshua. Mahogany seemed really happy and her husband, Damien, appeared to be a man who will love her for the rest of her life. I understand where you're coming from, but know that you will find someone."

"I know," agreed Joshua. "I do wish her the…" Joshua stopped mid-sentence when he heard a thunderous trumpet sound.

"Do you hear that?" asked Pastor Ethan.

Both men vanished into the air, leaving their telephones and clothes crumbling to the floor. The Rapture had taken place.

*   *   *

Nicole activated her car alarm before strolling into the Phoenix Technology office building. Adrenaline rushed through her veins. Not only had she witnessed several car accidents as she pulled into the parking lot, but today she would sit in on the firing of Damien Andrews. The fact that he got married yesterday allowed her to feel a little less guilty for recommending his termination. It was nothing personal. She was simply following orders from Rome.

Nicole saw Mr. Reed rushing out of the building. "Michael, where are you going?"

"My wife just called from my son's day-care! He frantically yelled, "All the children are gone!" Nicole had never seen him so flustered.

"What do you mean 'gone'?"

"They've all just disappeared. My wife was holding our son's hand one minute and the next minute he was wasn't there. I've got to go find him, Nicole."

Leaving her behind, Michael ran to his car. Following her gut instincts, Nicole rushed inside to call David. People were already gathered around the television in the lobby watching the news, a reporter's shaky voice echoed in the building.

"This unexplainable phenomenon has taken place all over the world. People and children have simply vanished into thin air. Many countries around the world have declared a state of emergency. Millions of car wrecks have been reported and we are facing a shortage of policemen, fireman, and doctors. It is a major problem of epic proportions. To describe this situation as chaotic would be a gross understatement. The burning questions that need to be answered are: What in God's name happened? And where did everyone go?"

Nicole took the elevator up to her office. Once exiting the elevator, she shut the door and dialed David. All the phone lines were jammed. It took her ten minutes to finally get through to him.

"David, what is happening? Have you seen the news?"

"I have, Nicole and all I can tell you is to keep watching the television. It will all make sense when we hear from him. Don't worry. Calm your fears. He will comfort all your worries. Listen, dear, I can't talk long. I must go."

Nicole listened as the line went dead. What the hell? David did not answer one of her questions. She tried calling her parents and other family members and received no answer. A cold chill seeped into her bones. She was scared. She followed David's advice and turned on the television. Observing the video from around the world caused a knot to form in the pit of Nicole's stomach. For the first time in her life, she was terrified of the future.

*   *   *

It was night time in Russia. From his office, Vladimir watched international news journalists report on the worldwide disappearances.

The news reports were music to his ears. He interpreted the disappearances as a sign to move ahead with the clandestine attack against the United States. Undoubtedly, the United States guard was down, more so than before. He placed a call to General Bolshoy. Vladimir gave the final order to execute operation Broken Eagle. Relaxing in his chair, Vladimir placed a second call to his wife, letting her know that he would be unable to make dinner. Tonight was going to be a very long one.

Minutes after giving the order, Vladimir watched the submarine surveillance video stream onto his computer screen. The nuclear missiles were unleashed within a matter of minutes. Los Angeles, New York, and Washington D.C. did not stand a chance against the fury of the radioactive bombs. Each city was immediately disintegrated. Combined with the unexplained disappearances and the devastating assaults, the United States lost tens of millions of people. Historians recorded this day in their books. In less than an hour, the United States of America lost her super-power crown and became a third-world country.

*   *   *

"Citizens of the world, I know that many of you are frightened by today's events and are concerned about the future of the world that we are currently living in. A war has broken out and millions of our loved ones have gone missing. I have used my position as President of the New Republic of Babylon to discover and unearth the truth surrounding these unexplained disappearances," Abdullah dramatically cleared his throat, "and what I'm about to tell you will be difficult and even hard to believe. But what I tell you is the reality of the situation. A team working at our International Space Station has deciphered radio frequency messages that were sent at the exact time of the disappearances. It reads as follows, 'There is life outside of your universe and we have taken millions of people from your world. Do not be concerned, for your loved ones are safe.' Ladies and gentlemen, we have no choice but to trust this information and wait to see if our love ones will be returned. The shocking attack upon the United States has completely unhinged our world economy. Prior to these horrendous events, the International Quartet advised the transfer of the United Nations headquarters to Babylon, I propose we now follow their advice. I can't think of anything more than moving our world organization to a land that would stimulate and stabilize our global economy. I swear to you, I will personally oversee each detail until mankind is commercially stable as it was before this calamity befell us. In the meantime, I am requesting that everyone get tagged with an R.F.I.D chip so that the government can find you in case our citizens go missing," he finished. He knew people would have no problem believing the lie told about the aliens. Ever since the Roswell alien crash, people were infatuated with U.F.O.'s.

Abdullah Hakeem gave a signal to stop the cameras from rolling. The final curtain had risen and now it was time for him to take his part onto the world's stage. All the chips were in place. He credited Pope David who laid the initial ground work. Abdullah was a grand military leader. When first given his assignment, he did not fully understand how he could hold the entire world under his sway. In the coming days, anyone who wished to buy or sell would bear his mark, name, or number in allegiance to him, Abdullah Hakeem.

Woe to any person who refused to swear loyalty to him. His trusted prophet, Pope David, would ensure that they would meet their fate. He smiled to himself thinking about the consequences of those who chose to refuse to do so. Beheadings offered a quick death…yes, the guillotine would definitely return from the past.

The Christians were finally gone. He smiled to himself in satisfaction. They would have warned the others of his true identity—the Son of Perdition, otherwise known as the Antichrist. With their removal, Abdullah would have free reign and absolute control over the affairs of mankind. Those who missed the rapture were now his puppets and at the end of his play, not only would he cut off their strings, but lead mankind directly to the gates of Hell.